Zoey Lyndon
and the
Sticky Finger Bandit

First Edition
Printed in the United States

Library of Congress Control Number:
2021909811

ISBN: 978-1-7366167-0-3 (paperback)
ISBN: 978-1-7366167-1-0 (eBook)
ISBN: 978-1-7366167-2-7 (hardback)

Illustrations by Lara Calleja

Published by:
JOA Press
Seminole, FL

Zoey Lyndon
and the
Sticky Finger Bandit

Micheal Anderson

Chapter 1

Who's The Culprit

You've gotta be kidding me! Ugh. I can't believe someone took my pencil—AGAIN! That's the second time this month.

Zoey Lyndon growled under her breath in frustration. She grabbed the pencil case from her desk and took out a new pencil. *At least I don't have to worry about anyone taking my case,* she thought. Her mom had written her name on it with a marker, and a fuzzy ball keychain hung from the zipper.

She kept her pencil stored in the front of her desk so that it was easily accessible. A couple of weeks ago, she thought she lost the one with a unicorn on it. But she hadn't moved it, so someone must have taken it. Now, she had a new set of motivational pencils her mom bought her and the one that said *Be Happy* had gone missing too! Recently, multiple items had vanished from Mrs. Pennington's—aka Mrs. P's—fourth grade classroom, and she wanted the students to let her know the next time something disappeared.

Zoey raised her hand and blurted, "Mrs. P, someone took another pencil out of my desk!" She huffed in exasperation.

"Zoey, are you sure you haven't misplaced it? Try checking your backpack," Mrs. P asked, trying to hide her irritation.

"I know I didn't misplace it because I used it this morning before we went to the library."

"Okay, Zoey! What does it look like?"

"It's light blue and it says *Be Happy.*"

Mrs. P asked the class if anyone had Zoey's pencil. Everyone responded by shaking their head and saying no, not me, or uh-uh. She told Zoey to use another one for now and assured her that hers would turn up later.

"Class, please pull out your math textbook and turn to page eighty-four."

Zoey was still irritated, but she pulled out her textbook and followed along as they practiced one and two-digit division. They were just starting to learn about dividing with remainders. Since Zoey's favorite subjects were science and math, she didn't mind these exercises. Mrs. P passed out a worksheet that had twelve problems—some with remainders and some without.

After the class completed the worksheets and turned them in, it was time for lunch. As the students lined up to go to the cafeteria, Zoey grabbed her monogrammed lunch box and joined the line with her friends Tommi, Emily, and Olivia.

The cafeteria was loud as always. Tommi and Zoey told their friends they would save them a seat at their usual table, since most of the time they packed their lunch. Tommi Mitchell was Zoey's bestie and also the first friend she made when she transferred to Briar Ridge Elementary at the beginning of the school year.

Emily and Olivia made it through the lunch line faster than usual and joined them at the table.

Emily asked her friends, "Does anyone want to perform in the talent show?"

Posters promoting Briar Ridge Elementary's annual talent show hung in practically every hallway of the school.

"Oh yeah, I saw the posters and I was thinking about signing up," Tommi replied. "Oh, wait a minute. Wouldn't it be great if we entered as a girl group and came up with a dance or something!" Her voice was high with excitement.

Olivia agreed. "Oh my God! We should totally do it! We can call ourselves the Diva Squad or something like that."

"Sounds like a good idea to me. We might have to come up with a better name for our group though," Zoey chimed.

Emily blurted, "We could call ourselves the Glitz Girls!"

Zoey was not surprised with the name Emily suggested, because her favorite color was pretty much anything pink and glittery. Every day she wore something shimmery. Today, her ensemble consisted of a white tee shirt with hot pink, sparkly letters that spelled out *Girls Rock* and a denim skirt with pink glitter speckled throughout. A pair of silver and pink dangly earrings hung from her ears and jingled every time she turned her head.

"How about we all come up with a name for our group, and we can decide tomorrow?" Zoey opened her bag of tiny pretzels and took one out.

The girls all agreed. Tommi suggested they decide if they were going to sing or dance.

"Who wants to sing?" Olivia asked.

The girls looked at one another, but no one spoke a word.

Olivia tapped her chin. "Okay then, who thinks we should dance?"

Zoey raised her hand. "I do." She grabbed another pretzel and took a bite. Tommi and Emily agreed. The girls talked about music and what song they might dance to. Then somehow the subject changed to the classroom culprit. Within the last couple of months, several students had personal items stolen from their desks or backpacks. At first no one thought anything of it, and the students assumed they had misplaced their things. But after a while, it became obvious someone in class had developed a case of sticky fingers.

It started when Josh Hightower had two dollars taken from his desk. He had brought in the money to buy extra snacks at lunch time. Then, Tommi's candy bar went missing from her backpack. Granted, the candy bar had been sticking out of its front pocket, but it still should have been safe. Next, Olivia's butterfly eraser disappeared. And now, Zoey's two pencils.

Still irritated about her missing pencils, Zoey said, "Who knows what else the sticky finger bandit has taken? They got me twice this month." Her hazel eyes flashed in anger. "Mrs. P should have stopped the class and demanded that everyone open their backpacks."

"Who do you think it is?" Emily asked as she stood up and gathered her trash.

"I have no idea," Tommi said, closing her lunch box.

Mrs. P walked to the entrance of the cafeteria, which meant lunchtime was over. The girls wracked their brains, trying to determine who the sticky finger bandit could be. But they would have to figure that out later, because it was time to go back to class.

They walked to their classroom and took their seats. Mrs. P stood at the front and said, "Please take your seat and pull out your spelling book. Let's review lesson fourteen before your test on Friday." She looked at Tommi. "Tomasina, spell the word *groceries* and use it in a sentence."

Tommi scrunched up her face. She didn't like being called by her full name. She spelled out, "G-R-O-C-E-R-I-E-S. My mom asked me to help bring in the groceries."

"Good job!" Mrs. P encouraged Tommi with a slight nod of her head.

"Jackson, spell the word *ancient* and use it in a sentence please."

Jackson spelled out, "A-N-C-I-E-N-T. My dad's farts smell ancient."

The classroom erupted in laughter, and Jackson laughed so hard that his face turned red.

"All right now—that's enough of that!" Mrs. P said, giving Jackson the stank face. Her nostrils flared and lifted the left side of her top lip.

She continued to give each student a word from their spelling list. Afterward, she had them close their spelling books and gave them a pop quiz.

Once they completed their quiz, the students graded their own papers as she called out the proper spelling of each word. As usual, Mrs. P gave the students two extra words they hadn't reviewed. They received extra points if they spelled the words correctly and could use them in a sentence.

Later that afternoon when Zoey got home from school, she dropped her backpack at the bottom of the stairs and headed to the kitchen to get a snack.

Zoey's older sister, Jasmine, always got home before Zoey. She sat at the kitchen table, eating a grilled cheese sandwich.

"Hey, Zo!"

"Hey, Jazz! Wassup?"

Their mom entered the room from the hallway. "Zoey, would you like a grilled cheese?"

"Yes, please!" Zoey answered, glad she didn't have to find something to eat on her own.

Her mom took a pack of cheddar cheese out of the refrigerator, then pointed out that Zoey still needed to carry her backpack upstairs to her room.

Zoey wondered how in the heck her mom even knew she had left it at the bottom of the steps. *She must have eyes in the back of her head.*

She left the kitchen. When she returned, her grilled cheese sandwich waited for her on the table. Her mother had cut it diagonally, just the way she liked.

"So, how was your day?" Zoey asked her sister before taking a bite of her warm and gooey sandwich.

"I think I have a secret admirer," Jasmine stated casually, leaning back in her chair.

"Oh, really!" Zoey's eyes lit up with intrigue. "Who do you think it is?"

Jasmine shrugged. "I don't know! I found a note on my desk in history class today, and next to the note was a chocolate kiss."

"And you didn't see who left it for you?"

"No, Zo, I didn't. When I got to class, I went to hand in my homework. When I went back to my desk, the note and chocolate kiss were already there. It must be someone from history class."

"So, what did the note say?" Zoey asked.

"Seriously! I swear—you are so nosey!"

Zoey rolled her eyes. "Oh, stop being a meanie! What did it say?"

Shaking her head, Jasmine replied, "It said, *Jasmine, I think you're cute. Do you have a boyfriend?*"

Excitement bubbled in Zoey's chest. "Uh oh. Looks like Noah has some competition."

Noah was Jasmine's best friend's older brother. He was in the eighth grade and was sweet on Jasmine.

Jasmine gave a loud exaggerated sigh and an eye roll. She walked away from the table, leaving Zoey alone.

Zoey shrugged and continued eating her grilled cheese. She wasn't surprised that two boys liked her sister. Jasmine's flawless mocha complexion, thick wavy hair, and easy smile made her a natural beauty. She was the type of girl that was drop dead gorgeous and acted as if she didn't notice, which only made people like her even more.

After Zoey finished her snack, she headed upstairs to her room to start her homework. She also wanted to come up with a list of possible names for their dance group for the talent show and to think of at least one or two good songs. She and her friends had planned to finalize the name of the group and to pick a song tomorrow at lunch. The sooner they decided, the sooner they could start to practice. The talent show was in six weeks, and the girls were going to need all that time to get their dance routine together. No one wanted to look stupid in front of the entire school.

Zoey looked at the clock on her nightstand next to her bed and couldn't believe it was already close to six o'clock. She finished her homework and watched YouTube videos to get ideas for their routine. She finally found two upbeat songs she thought would be great. Beyonce's song, "Before I Let Go," was popular. Zoey remembered even the adults had enjoyed it when they played it at the family cookout that summer. The other song, "Mi Gente" by J. Balvin and Willy William, was high energy and a lot of fun. She hoped her friends would like her choices.

Tuesdays in the Lyndon household were known as Taco Tuesday. You could have your choice of hard or soft-shell tacos, and her mom always made Spanish rice as a side dish.

Zoey went downstairs to the kitchen. Her mom and dad already sat at the table with their dinner in front of them.

Her mom placed her napkin in her lap. "Zoey, please tell your sister it's time to eat."

Zoey pulled out a chair at the dinner table to take a seat. "I already told her, but she's on her phone."

Her mother stared at her with her signature raised eyebrow and repeated herself. But this time she emphasized each word. "Go get your sister and tell her it's time to eat."

Zoey sighed, pushed the chair back, and turned to get her sister. But Jasmine came down the stairs and into the room just in time.

Their dad looked up from his plate and teased, "Hurry up slow poke. Food's getting cold."

Zoey sat down, and Jasmine smiled and took the seat across from her.

"Hey, Daddy!" She put the ingredients for her soft-shell taco and a scoop of rice onto her plate.

"So, how was everyone's day?" Their father asked in his booming voice, while shoveling more rice onto his fork.

"Me and my friends are going to be in the school talent show," Zoey replied.

"Oh, really? That sounds fun. What are you girls going to do?" Her mother asked.

"We're going to do a dance routine," she answered excitedly.

Jasmine chuckled. "What song are you going to dance to?"

"We don't know yet. We're going to decide tomorrow. Everyone is supposed to come up with a group name and a song, and we'll pick the best one. I chose *Quad Squad* for the name and "Mi Gente" by J. Balvin and Willy William for our song. Or maybe Beyonce's "Before I Let Go.""

"Oh, I like "Mi Gente!" That one is upbeat, and you can get the crowd into it to hype you guys up," Jasmine said.

Dad chimed, "I don't think I know either one of those songs."

"Well, I know Beyonce's," their mom said. "I like that one. I don't think I know the other one, but as long as you girls have fun. Good luck!"

Jasmine announced, "We are having a school dance next Friday night. It's called the Winter Snow Ball."

Her mom's face lit up, and she turned her attention to her eldest daughter. "Aw—my baby's first big girl dance!"

Dad smiled proudly. "And she is going to be the prettiest girl there." He said as he took a bite of his third taco.

"Thank you, Daddy. But you have to say that because I'm your daughter," Jasmine pointed out, shaking her head.

"Who are you going to go to the dance with?" Zoey asked.

Jasmine held up her index finger and finished chewing her mouthful of rice before answering. "Aubrey and I are going solo and will meet up with some of our friends when we get there."

"Well, it looks like we are going shopping this weekend," their mother insisted.

The smile on Jasmine's face told Zoey how excited she was. *She must be looking forward to her first dance.*

Her mom quickly shifted gears into Operation Glam. "I'll make you a hair appointment first thing tomorrow. I want to make sure I can get you in with my stylist before your big night. And I'll do your makeup."

"Makeup," their dad barked. "She doesn't need any makeup."

"Well of course she doesn't need it, silly," she chastised. "It will merely enhance her natural beauty."

They continued talking about the Winter Snow Ball as they finished their dinner. After, the girls cleaned the kitchen and put away the dishes, Zoey shared her suspicions with Jasmine about the classroom culprit.

"So, we seem to have a thief in our class. A lot of things have gone missing lately."

Jasmine gave her a curious look. "What type of things?"

"Josh had his lunch money taken from his desk, Tommi had a Hershey bar taken from her backpack, Olivia had an eraser stolen, and I've had two pencils disappear—including one of the new ones that mom just bought me."

"Aw man, Zo. It sure does sound like someone has been stealing from you guys," Jasmine replied, shaking her head in disbelief. "Make sure you start keeping your things at the back of your desk or in your backpack so they can't take anything else from you."

"Mrs. P told us to let her know when it happens again, and I think she is on the lookout. The crazy thing is no one knows who the thief is."

"Well, if they keep it up, they are going to get caught." Jasmine said.

After they finished cleaning the kitchen, Jasmine went to hang out with their dad in the family room. Zoey went to see what her mom was up to.

She strolled into her mother's office. "Hey Mom, whatcha doin'?" She plopped into the chair in front of her mother's desk.

Her mom looked up from her computer. "I'm working on a piece for the business journal. What do you need, Zo?"

Realizing her mother probably had a deadline to meet, Zoey got up to leave and told her she didn't really want anything.

Her mom tilted her head. "Are you sure?"

"I was just going to ask if you could help me and my friends with our dance for the talent show?"

"Of course. I would love to." Her mother's face brightened. "That won't be a problem at all. In fact, this will give me a chance to dust off my dance skills. How about we talk about it more once I finish writing my article and you decide on the song?"

"Sounds good to me! I'll get out of your hair so you can finish your work," Zoey responded. "See ya later!"

She got to her feet and left her mother's office, excited to have her help with the routine. Zoey's mother had been on the dance team at a HBCU (a Historical Black College and University) and was an excellent dancer. With her help, the girls would definitely have a real shot at taking first place.

Zoey went upstairs to her room and started getting ready for bed.

"Knock knock!" Jasmine leaned against the doorway. "Hey, Zo. I was just thinking you should probably ask Mom to help you and your girls choreograph a dance routine for your talent show. You know how she is always talking about back in the day when she was on the dance team at CSU (Central State University)."

Zoey nodded in agreement. "I know, right? I just talked to her, and she said she would help."

"Ah. Glad that worked out for you. You guys are gonna kick butt. Night, Zo!" Jasmine gave Zoey a little smile, then headed to her room.

"Good night, Jazz!" Zoey called out. She turned out her light and got into bed, ready to dream about her cool new dance routine with her friends.

Chapter 2

Gym Class Debacle

The next morning, Zoey couldn't wait to get to school so she and her friends could decide on the name of their dance group and the song they were going to dance to.

She put away her jacket and backpack and quickly found her seat. Mrs. P stood at the front of the room, wearing a pair of black and white, gingham high-waist pants and a cute black sweater with a white collar. Zoey always looked forward to seeing what Mrs. P wore— she usually has the cutest clothes.

Mrs. P greeted her students as they entered the classroom. She instructed, "Please find your seat so we can complete our reading lesson before gym class this morning."

She took attendance, made the usual morning announcements, and then got started on the reading lesson. She had the students read a story about the first two men that climbed Mount Everest in 1953. After, she asked them questions pertaining to what they read to help them develop strong comprehensive skills. Once reading was over, she had them get ready for gym class.

"Alright, please put your things away and line up at the door."

They walked the short distance down the hall and around the corner to the gymnasium. Mr. Lockwood, the gym teacher at Briar Ridge Elementary, had the students count off and form teams. All of the ones were on a team, and all of the twos were on the other.

Zoey and Emily were on Team One with Josh Hightower and Jackson Smith. They were playing dodgeball today—Zoey hated that game because some of the kids threw the ball way too hard. Emily and Zoey tried to stay back in the corner or behind Josh and Jackson, so they wouldn't get hit. They were both doing a good job of dodging the ball when all of a sudden—WHAM!!!

"OH MY GOD! Zoey, are you okay?" Josh asked, with panic in his voice.

Zoey literally saw stars! She stood there, trying to hold back the tears quickly puddling in her eyes. It was as if he spoke in slow motion, and she wasn't able to find her words.

Trudy Jacobs had hit her in the face. Yes, Trudy was a girl. But she certainly didn't look like a fourth grader. With her towering height, and fully developed boobs, she looked like she should be in sixth grade. Zoey had been standing behind Josh. When he had suddenly ducked at the last minute, the ball hit her dead in the face. She never saw it coming.

Zoey couldn't hold back the tears any longer because her face felt like it was on fire. Her friends were talking to her, but she couldn't formulate her words because she was in so much pain.

"I'm sorry Zoey, if I hadn't ducked then you wouldn't have gotten hit," Josh insisted.

Mr. Lockwood hurried over to them. "Zoey are you okay?"

Since Zoey's face felt as if it was burning, she could only shake her head no.

"Emily, walk Zoey down to nurse Murphy's office. I think she may need an ice pack," Mr. Lockwood instructed.

By the time Emily and Zoey reached the nurse's office, Zoey had started to compose herself and was finally able to talk again. With Emily by her side, she approached the nurse's desk and let out a whimper.

Emily blurted, "Nurse Murphy, Trudy Jacobs hit Zoey in the face while we were playing dodgeball in gym class."

Nurse Murphy stood from her chair and walked over to Zoey to get a look at her injury. "Have a seat, Zoey. Let's get you an ice pack—you can hold on your cheek to help with the swelling."

She walked to the refrigerator in the corner and took out a small ice pack, then handed it to Zoey and told her to lie down on the cot for a little while.

Zoey stretched out—and closed her eyes. She was thankful for the relief the ice pack provided. It was cold, but it was also soothing and felt good.

"Emily dear," said Nurse Murphy, "you can go on back to class. I will send Zoey back to Mrs. Pennington's room later."

They were in the middle of learning the state capitals for the southeast states when Zoey came back from the nurse's office. Mrs. P told her what page they were on and continued with the lesson. Once they finished their social studies, she reminded her class that the last day to sign up for the school talent show was Friday. After she answered a few questions, she had the student's line up for lunch.

Once they got to the lunchroom, Zoey said to Olivia and Emily, "We'll see you guys at the table."

She and Tommi went to sit at their regular spot. Both girls usually packed their lunch, which made it easy for them to save seats for their friends. Zoey had her usual turkey sandwich with a slice of cheese, pretzel sticks, and an apple. She always brought her own personal bottle of hot sauce in her lunch box, and her classmates would often ask to borrow it.

They took their seats and opened their lunches. "What did you pack today?" Zoey asked Tommi.

"Mini tacos, a bag of Doritos, and orange slices," Tommi answered as she tore open a packet of taco sauce.

Zoey poured a few drops of hot sauce onto her turkey sandwich. "Your mini tacos look good."

"Umm—they are good." Tommi answered, her mouth full. "Does your face still hurt?" She asked with concern.

Just as she was getting ready to answer, Olivia and Emily sat down.

"What'd we miss?" Olivia asked, then took a bite of her hamburger.

"Nothing. I was just telling Tommi that I feel better now. The ice pack Nurse Murphy gave me really helped."

"I'm glad it didn't leave a mark on your face," Tommi said.

Emily chimed in, "Well apparently Tommi and Trudy got into it after we left gym class."

Zoey put down her sandwich. "Hold up—Wait a minute—What happened?"

"You missed it! Tommi told Trudy off after you guys left." Olivia huffed.

"Tommi got up in Trudy's face and asked, what was her problem? And Trudy told her ... *I don't have a problem*." Olivia said.

Tommi chimed in, "I asked her why she didn't apologize for hitting you in the face with the ball and she had the nerve to say that '*She didn't have to apologize because it was an accident*.' I told her, everyone knew that, but she could've still said she was sorry."

"Then she got up in Tommi's face and told her '*I don't have to apologize, and you can't make me*!' Tommi looked her dead in the eye and said '*You wanna bet?*'" Olivia spouted.

"Yeah, and that's when Mr. Lockwood came over and told us to break it up." Tommi stated.

"No way!" Zoey sat on the edge of her seat in disbelief. "I can't believe I missed all the action!"

"Olivia spoke up, "We all know that Trudy is not a nice person. But right now, we need to talk about something more important. Like the talent show. Did y'all come up with a name for our group and a song for us to dance to?"

The girls shared the different names they all thought of for their group. Emily liked Glitz Girls, Zoey suggested Quad Squad, Tommi recommended Divine Divas, and Olivia came up with Fly Girls. It was a toss-up between Glitz Girls and Fly Girls, but they ended up choosing Glitz Girls.

The only song that all the girls could agree on was Zoey's suggestion, "Mi Gente."

"Now that we've chosen a name and selected our song, we need to decide when we are going to start practicing," said Tommi.

"I asked my mom last night if she would help us, and she agreed that she would. She went to a HBCU and was on the dance team," Zoey said proudly.

Olivia gave Zoey a confused look and questioned, "What's a HBCU?"

"A HBCU is a Historical Black College or University," Zoey explained.

"Yeah, I think my dad went to a HBCU. We used to watch some of their college football games together when he still lived with us," Tommi said.

Tommi's parents were divorced, but since they lived in the same city, she got to spend time with both of them regularly.

"So, when do y'all want to start practicing?" Emily asked, then took the last bite of her hamburger.

"Well, since we only have about six weeks before the talent show, maybe we should start this weekend," Zoey pointed out.

Her friends all agreed.

"This weekend should be fine, but I need to doublecheck with my mom to make sure it will work for her. I will let you know what she says tomorrow," Zoey promised.

Emily and Olivia threw away their lunch plates while Tommi and Zoey zipped up their lunch boxes, ready to go back to class. Mrs. P stood at the entrance to the cafeteria talking to another teacher as she gestured to her students that it was time to go. Her class lined up in single file and headed back to class.

When they got back to their room, Mrs. P gave them twenty minutes of indoor recess, because it was cold outside. Most of the students went to grab their video games or comic books, and a few went to the cupboard to pull out Mrs. P's board games. Zoey usually read at her desk during indoor recess, but today she forgot to bring her book. Instead, she sat quietly talking to Josh, Tommi, and Jackson. The boys only half paid attention because they were focused on their Nintendo Switch video games.

"So, have you decided what you're going to do for your birthday yet?" Jackson asked Josh, keeping his eyes on his game.

"Yeah, my mom agreed that I can have a Laser Tag party at Sports Fusion," Josh answered excitedly.

"Awe man—that is so cool!" Jackson replied.

Zoey asked jokingly, "So am I invited?"

Josh smiled. "Of course, silly. My mom told me to invite the whole class, but I was always going to invite you and your squad."

"Ooh—that's nice!" Tommi said. "When is your party?

"Next Sunday."

"Oh no! On Sundays our family always goes to church." Zoey pouted.

"Maybe you can do both. My party doesn't start until one o'clock." Josh jabbed at his Switch controller with his thumb.

"Okay, that will work! We usually go to the early morning service, and we should definitely be home by then."

Jackson and Josh talked about their games, while Tommi and Zoey discussed the school talent show.

Once recess was over, Mrs. P had the class put their things away to review for the spelling test they were having the next day. She also added a grammar lesson before it was time to go home. The bell rang, and the students put away their books and packed up their backpacks, then Mrs. P dismissed them. Zoey walked outside with the bus riders to meet her mom, who waited for her in the car line. Since Mrs. Lyndon worked from home, Zoey never had to ride the school bus.

Once Zoey got in the passenger seat, her mom examined her face. She grabbed Zoey's chin and turned her face left and to the right, so she could get a good look at her.

"Doesn't look like you have any bruising," she said. "How do you feel?"

Zoey rubbed her cheek. "Surprisingly, I feel fine. When I got hit with the ball, it felt like my face was on fire. I wanted to come home, but after

Nurse Murphy gave me an ice pack and let me lie down for a while, I felt a lot better."

Zoey's mom put the car in drive and pulled out onto the street. "I'm certainly glad Nurse Murphy called me, because I was ready to come and pick you up. But she assured me that you were doing well, so I decided it was okay for you to remain at school. So, what happened?"

"We were playing dodgeball, and Trudy Jacobs tried to hit Josh and ended up hitting me in the face instead. I know it was an accident, but she never even apologized."

Zoey's mom glanced at her and shook her head. "Well, I'm glad you are okay."

They were quiet for the rest of the drive home. Once her mom parked the car, Zoey jumped out and ran into the house, looking for her sister.

"Jazz! Where are you?" She wanted to tell Jazz about her crazy day.

"In the kitchen," Jasmine yelled back.

Zoey ran upstairs to drop her backpack in her room, then headed to the kitchen for a snack.

Jasmine sat at the table, eating pizza bagels.

"You are not going to believe what happened to me today!" Zoey took some pizza bagels from the box on the counter and put them into the microwave.

"What happened?" Jasmine asked.

Zoey poured herself a glass of water and waited for the microwave to beep. "One second." She took her snack, grabbed a napkin, and then sat down across from Jasmine. "When we were in gym class today, I got hit in the face with a dodgeball."

"Oh my God! Are you okay?" Jasmine asked with genuine concern.

"Yeah, I'm fine now, but I wanted to cry like a baby when it happened." Zoey sighed, then took a bite of a pepperoni pizza bagel.

"Well, I'm glad you're alright."

"Apparently, I missed all the drama that happened after I went to the nurse's office though."

Her sister cocked her head and raised an eyebrow. "What do you mean by that? What happened?"

Zoey gave her a rundown of the Tommi & Trudy drama that ensued and how Mr. Lockwood had to break it up before it went any further.

"Wow! That's crazy!" Jasmine replied. "But besides that, did you girls decide on a name for your dance group?"

"Yep, the Glitz Girls." Zoey said. "And we're dancing to 'Mi Gente.'"

Changing the subject, Zoey asked, "So, do you know who your secret admirer is yet?"

Jasmine pushed her now-empty plate aside. "Nope. Not yet. Although, I did find another note in my chair in history class."

Zoey's eyes went wide as she leaned closer to her sister, not wanting to miss any of the juicy info. "What did it say?"

Jasmine chuckled. "I swear you are the nosiest little sister—ever. It's none of your business, Miss Nosey Pants."

Zoey kicked the leg of the table. "Ugh! I swear—I don't know why you are so secretive? It's not like I'm going to tell anybody."

"I do tell you stuff, but you don't need to know all of my business." Jasmine stuck out her tongue. "Besides, you tell Tommi everything."

Jasmine continued to sit and chat while Zoey finished eating her snack. One of the rules in the

Lyndon household was that the girls only had forty-five minutes of downtime before they had to start their homework. This was just enough time to watch an episode of one of their favorite shows on Netflix, *Absolute Drama*—an animated show about the adventures and mishaps of a group of teenagers. Each episode was thirty minutes long, so the girls had just enough time to watch it after their snack. After that, it was time to hit the books.

The girls headed upstairs to their bedrooms to tackle their homework.

After focusing on her math, Zoey glanced at the clock on her nightstand. It was already a quarter after six—almost time for dinner. *Geesh, where has the time gone?* She only had a comprehension worksheet left to complete, and then she needed to study for her spelling.

"Time to eat!" Mrs. Lyndon called from downstairs.

Jasmine and Zoey ran down the stairs and to the kitchen. Mr. Lyndon was already setting the table around the baked chicken, green beans, rolls, and a big pitcher of lemonade. Mrs. Lyndon took her seat and helped herself to a drumstick.

"Umm—smells good, Mom," Jasmine said as she sat across from her.

"Hey, Daddy, when did you get home?" Zoey sat next to Jasmine, then poured herself a glass of lemonade.

"About thirty minutes ago." He placed a bowl of seasoned potatoes on the table, then sat in his spot next to his wife.

Dinner had always been a time when the Lyndon family would gather around the table and discuss the events of the day. The kitchen was filled with laughter and conversation as they all had the opportunity to share the details of their daily lives.

"Mom, we picked out the name of our dance group." Zoey heaped some potatoes onto her plate. "We are the *Glitz Girls,* and we are gonna dance to 'Mi Gente.' Do you think we can start working on our routine this weekend?" She added a chicken leg, green beans, and a dinner roll next to her potatoes.

"Sure, we can get started on Saturday afternoon."

"Okay, cool! What time should I tell my friends?"

"How about three o'clock? This way, everyone has time to attend their regular activities and get all of their errands out of the way," her mom answered.

Zoey told her Dad about the dodgeball debacle and brought both parents up to speed on the Tommi and Trudy shenanigans. She was glad she got to use one of her spelling words in a sentence— she hadn't even known what debacle meant before this week. It was even one of the extra credit spelling words from Mrs. P.

"Oh, Mom, Aubrey wants to know if I can sleep over at her house next Saturday." Jasmine said.

Their mom looked at their dad, who shrugged his shoulders and took his second piece of chicken.

Mrs. Lyndon shrugged. "I don't have a problem with it, as long as her parents don't have an issue with you staying over."

"Thanks, Mom!" Jasmine said.

Zoey remembered Josh's invitation and turned to her mom. "Oh, before I forget, Josh Hightower is having a birthday party next Sunday at some laser tag place. The whole class was invited."

Her mother pursed her lips. "Now, you know we have church on Sunday. What time is the party?"

"It's not until one o'clock, and since we always go to the early service, we should be home in plenty of time for me to go."

Zoey's mother didn't play when it came to church. The only time that Zoey ever got out of going was if she was sick or the roads were too bad. When they lived in Philly, sometimes they would get so much snow that they would cancel church due to inclement weather. She didn't know how the winters were going to be here in Missouri, but she doubted they would get as much snow as they got back in Philadelphia.

"In that case, we don't have a problem with it," her mom replied.

The Lyndons finished up dinner, and the girls began to clear off the table as usual. Because their mom was a freelance writer who worked from home, they always had home-cooked meals. The only exception was Fridays—which were pizza night, Saturdays—when their mom didn't cook at all, or special occasions when they would go out to eat.

Once the girls finished cleaning the kitchen, they watched a couple of episodes of *Absolute Drama*, then Zoey made her way upstairs to finish her homework.

Chapter 3

The Glitz Girls Dance Rehearsal

Saturday mornings in the Lyndon household meant big breakfasts and household chores. After eating a hearty meal, Zoey and Jasmine headed upstairs to clean their rooms. Their dad was working on one of his many projects in the garage, while their mom was downstairs cleaning. The house always smelled of a mixture of lemon, lavender, and bleach on Saturdays.

Sounds of Stevie Wonder singing *"As,"* wafted through the house, blaring from the surround sound system.

After the bedrooms were cleaned, the floors had been swept and mopped, and the laundry had been put away, the girls were free to relax.

They bounded down the stairs to the kitchen, where their mom had just finished cleaning the stove. Jasmine hopped from one foot to the other. "Mom, can I go over to Aubrey's to hang out? Her mother is going to take us to the Galleria."

Their mom raised a brow. "Did you finish putting away your clothes?"

"Yes, ma'am. And I already finished my homework."

"In that case, I don't mind, but I don't want you going over there all of the time. She is more than welcome to come over here."

"Oh, I know," Jasmine replied. "The only reason I'm going over there is because I knew that Zoey's classmates were coming over, and I didn't want to be around her silly little friends."

In an amused voice, her mother replied, "I understand. Do you need me to take you over there?"

"No. Her mom will pick me up and drop me back off.

"Okay then, sounds good to me." Their mom glanced down at her stained t-shirt. "I better go and get myself together before Zoey's friends get here," she said with a smile and headed upstairs to take a quick shower.

A few minutes later, the doorbell rang. *Ding Dong. Ding Dong.*

Zoey ran to open the door. "Mom!" She yelled. "They're here!" She swung it open and held it for them. "Hey, c'mon in."

Mrs. Lyndon came up and stood behind Zoey. Tommi and Emily's mothers stepped inside, followed by their daughters.

"Hello, Tonya, it's so good to see you again." Mrs. Lyndon welcomed Tommi's mom, who was dropping off Tommi and Olivia, with a friendly hug. She extended her hand to Emily's mother and gave her a warm smile. "Hello, I'm Rachel."

"Hello, Rachel. I'm Elle Stewart, Emily's mom." She smiled as she shook Rachel's hand. "Thank you so much for agreeing to do this for the girls. They are so excited about the talent show."

Tonya nudged Rachel playfully. "Are you sure you are up to this?"

"Absolutely! Ladies, I was on the dance team in college, and I'm certain that teaching our girls one routine will not be a problem."

Elle laughed. "I don't know. You haven't seen Emily dance."

"Trust me, ladies," Rachel said. "I'm sure the girls will all do fine. Plus, it's been a while since I was in full fledge dance mode—I think this might be fun."

Tonya asked, "Would you like for us to stay?"

"Oh, no. How about you pick them up in two hours?"

Tonya agreed to come back at five o'clock.

"Rachel, I am on my way to a meeting," Elle said. "But my husband, Matthew will be picking Emily up."

"Okay, thanks for letting me know. I look forward to meeting him."

They called for their daughters to tell them goodbye and told them what time they would see them later.

Now that the parents were gone, Rachel focused her attention on assessing each of the girl's raw talent. She knew that even though choreography can be taught, there are some people who pick up dance moves a lot quicker than others.

"Hey girls, let's go ahead and get started." Mrs. Lyndon guided them to the basement so they could have more room to dance.

The girls followed closely behind her, excited and wondered how easy the choreography would be.

"I want you all to spread out and put some space in between you. You are going to need room to move." Mrs. Lyndon clicked the remote to the Bose sound system, and the sound of "Mi Gente" pulsed throughout the basement.

The music was electric and had exciting energy. Mrs. Lyndon bobbed her head to the song, and Zoey could tell she liked it. The song just makes you want to dance.

With the music steady bumping, Mrs. Lyndon showed them a couple of basic moves. She did everything from the Moonwalk to the Milly Rock, which surprisingly they already knew how to do. Everyone liked the more popular dances like the Shoot and the Billy Bounce. Mrs. Lyndon taught the girls several dance moves with the traditional eight count.

After a few minutes of practice, Tommi let out a deep breath. "Oh my God, Zoey! Your mom is an amazing dancer."

"I was totally thinking the same thing." said Emily.

Olivia nodded in agreement.

"Girls, freestyle is when you simply make up your own moves doing whatever you want to do." Mrs. Lyndon demonstrated while snapping her fingers and moving her arms and hips to the rhythm of the music.

"Like this?" Emily asked as she bounced from side to side, working her shoulders with a little finger pop added on every beat.

"Yes, Emily. Just like that," Mrs. Lyndon said encouragingly.

After observing Tommi's impressive moves, she asked, "Where did you learn how to pop and lock like that?"

"My cousins on my Dad's side of the family are always having dance offs when we get together," she explained, still dancing with her hands in the air.

"How's this, Mrs. Lyndon?" Olivia asked, jumping around to a beat all of her own.

"Not bad!" She replied. "Freestyle is doing whatever you want to do. "We will work on staying on beat with the music though."

Zoey was dancing so hard she was almost out of breath. "Hey, Mom? Do you mind if we take a little break to grab a quick drink of water?"

Realizing that they had been at it for a little over an hour, Zoey's mom quickly agreed. "Oh, my word! I'm sorry girls. By all means, take a break and get something to drink."

Everyone was having such a good time that they didn't even notice they had worked up a sweat. They made their way up the stairs to the kitchen. After the girls sat at the table, Zoey gave them all a bottle of water from the fridge. She then grabbed herself a handful of green grapes that her Mom had set on the counter earlier that afternoon.

Her mom entered the kitchen and caught her eye. "Zoey! Where are your manners? Did you offer your friends some grapes?" She grabbed a glass from the cupboard above the sink and filled it with water from the tap.

"Sorry, Mom. I forgot," Zoey grumbled.

"Girls, please help yourselves to some grapes and then come back downstairs so we can finish up."

Olivia got up and took some grapes, then popped one into her mouth. "Ooh these taste like cotton candy!"

Emily and Tommi did the same.

"Yeah, these are good," Emily stated.

Tommi agreed with a nod and a, "Um hmm."

Mrs. Lyndon set her glass in the sink and pointed to the doorway. "Now that break time is over, let's see if we can put together a short combination."

They made their way back downstairs and took their places, ready to dance.

Zoey's mom stood in front of them and put her hands on her hips. "I think that this can be the opening to your routine, girls." She turned the music back on and began to count. "Five, six, seven, eight…"

She started showing them the combinations she wanted them to learn. Everyone was able to catch on quickly to the arrangement she put together.

"Good job, girls!" she said.

After going through the steps a few more times, the doorbell rang.

"Okay, girls. That's a wrap." Zoey's mother turned off the music, which was playing on repeat, and went to answer the door.

Chapter 4

Science Week

The following week was National Science Week. Mrs. P shared with us different types of jobs in the science, technology, engineering, and math (STEM) fields. She talked about how there is a need for more women in the fields of engineering, computer science, mathematics, biological science, and physical science. She debunked the myth that girls' abilities in math and science are less significant than boys. Mrs. P told us that engineering and computer science jobs are two of the higher paying STEM positions. Only 21% of engineering majors are women and just 19% of computer science majors are women. Although this was interesting information, the most exciting part was the actual experiments that Mrs. P prepared for us.

We had a variety of hands-on science experiments planned for the week. On Monday there was the *Tornado in a Bottle*, on Tuesday, it was *Hot Ice*. But Zoey's absolute favorite experiment was on Thursday.

"I'm going to need everyone to get into groups so we can get started on today's science experiment. Today, we are making *Elephant Toothpaste*," Mrs. P instructed.

The students quickly went to their groups of four that they had worked in all week. Zoey was in a group with Josh Hightower, Grayson Pierce, and Trudy Jacob. Mrs. P gave each group a tray that had all the ingredients and tools the kids would need.

"Please layout your plastic tablecloths and put on your safety goggles."

Zoey and Trudy spread the plastic tablecloth over their table, set the bowl and utensils on top, and everybody put on their goggles.

Since the students had to work as a team, Trudy measured half a cup of hydrogen peroxide, and Josh added one tablespoon of dishwashing liquid and ten drops of blue food coloring to the plastic bowl. In a separate, smaller bowl, Zoey mixed the yeast and warm water and stirred it for about thirty seconds. Finally, Grayson placed the funnel over the water bottle with the hydrogen peroxide solution in it and poured the yeast mixture inside.

Immediately, blue foam poured from the top of the plastic bottle.

"WHOA!" Grayson's eyes grew huge.

"That is so cool!" Trudy said with a huge smile.

Josh suggested that they touch the foam as it oozed out of the bottle and onto the plastic.

Mrs. P shook her head. "You can't touch it. There could be residual hydrogen peroxide—H_2O_2—that could potentially irritate your skin."

"Well, that's a bummer," mumbled Josh.

Zoey agreed, because she wanted to touch it as well to see what it felt like. It was just foaming bubbles. It didn't look dangerous.

Mrs. P began to explain the science behind the experiment. "The yeast mixture acted as a catalyst, and it quickly broke down the molecules in the experiment. It caused the oxygen—O_2—to separate from the hydrogen peroxide—H_2O_2—and this is what created the foaming bubbles that oozed out of the bottle. Because it looks a little like toothpaste, they call this experiment *Elephant Toothpaste*."

"Why was the foam warm?" Zoey asked. She hadn't touched it, like Mrs. P said, but she did touch the plastic bottle filled with the ooze and it was toasty.

"Yeah, the bottle was warm, Trudy added.

Mrs. P gave them a proud smile. "Great observation! The experiment created what's called an exothermic reaction, which means to generate or create heat." She paused and looked over the classroom. Now, if everyone will please clean up your workstations. Put all supplies back on the trays and discard the water bottles and trash by wrapping them up in the plastic sheets."

As Zoey reached for the tray, so she could put the remaining supplies away, Trudy snatched it from her hands, causing blue food coloring to get on Zoey's lavender sweater.

"TRUDY! I swear, you don't have to be so mean!"

Irritated, she looked down at the blue stain seeping through her sweater to her t-shirt underneath. "Look what you did!"

"It's not my fault it spilled on you!" Trudy snapped.

"Actually, it *is* your fault, Trudy," Josh said. "If you hadn't pulled the tray out of Zoey's hand, she never would have spilled the food coloring."

"Oh, shut up, Josh! Of course, you're going to come to her defense—everyone knows that you're in love with Zoey!

Mrs. P's sharp voice cut through the air. "Trudy! You know we do not talk to one another that way in my classroom." She marched to their workstation, looked at each student and asked, "What seems to be the problem?"

Grayson spoke up. "Zoey picked up the tray to put the supplies away, and Trudy grabbed the tray out of her hands."

Pointing to the blue stain on her sweater, Zoey confirmed his story. "Yes, Mrs. P. And now I have a big stain on my sweater and shirt."

Mrs. P pursed her lips and shook her head. "I might be able to get that stain out."

Luckily, there was a sink in her classroom. She had Zoey follow her to it, then grabbed a toothbrush and stain remover from the cabinet beneath it. She put the stain remover on the toothbrush, wet it, and then dabbed the blue splotches on the fabric—Wallah! Just like that, the stains were gone.

After the science experiment, it was lunch time. Zoey had a big wet mark on her t-shirt and sweater, but at least the food coloring had come out.

"Everyone let's line up to go to the cafeteria," Mrs. P announced. "Trudy, I'd like to talk to you."

Trudy rolled her eyes and glanced over at Zoey before hanging back to walk with Mrs. P to the lunchroom.

Zoey and Tommi headed to their usual table, while Emily and Olivia went through the line to get their food.

They sat down, and Tommi let out a huff. "Seriously! I totally can't believe Trudy blurted out that Josh is in love with you!"

"I know. I was so embarrassed!" Zoey opened her lunch box and pulled out her sandwich, pretzels, fruit cup, and her small bottle of hot sauce. "I couldn't believe she said that. It's a good thing,

Mrs. P interrupted before it could get any worse. I swear, sometimes I can't stand her!"

Tommi pulled out her ham sandwich. "It's because she's a bully. She thinks that just because she's bigger than everyone else, she can do whatever she wants." She picked up Zoey's hot sauce and poured a few drops of it on her sandwich. "Ain't nobody afraid of that girl."

Just then, Emily and Olivia arrived at the table, chomping at the bits to add their two cents to the conversation.

Emily, in her denim jeggings, pink sparkly ballerina flats, and hot pink sweater put down her tray and sat next to Zoey. "I always thought that Josh liked Zoey."

Olivia sat across from her and was quick to disagree. "I don't think that Josh likes Zoey. I think Trudy said that just to be mean."

Zoey swallowed her bite of sandwich. "I agree with Olivia. I don't think Josh likes me. Trudy is just mean. I'm just glad that Mrs. P. was able to get the food coloring out of my sweater." Feeling flustered, she paused. "I haven't been able to look at Josh since Trudy blurted that out."

"Honestly, Zoey you don't have anything to be embarrassed about. Trudy wishes somebody liked her." Tommi joked, and the girls laughed.

They changed the subject to talk about how cool that day's science experiment was. They all enjoyed watching the yeast and warm water react with the hydrogen peroxide. No one expected the foam to explode out of the top of the water bottle. Everyone agreed that *Elephant Toothpaste* was the best experiment that week.

As Tommi finished her lunch, she asked, "Is everyone going to Josh's party this weekend?"

"I am," Emily replied.

Olivia closed her lunchbox. "Me too. I love laser tag."

Zoey tapped her fingers on the table nervously. "Well, I was looking forward to going to his party, but now I just hope it's not going to be awkward."

"What's going on down there?" Tommi pointed to the end of the lunch table.

Zoey followed her gaze. The boys sitting there were getting loud and rowdy. The kids at the cafeteria table stared at them, fascinated with Jackson Smith for some reason.

Zoey called out, "Hey, what's going on?"

Grayson laughed boisterously. "Jackson is seeing how much ham he can stick up his nose. He is up to half a slice."

Zoey shook her head in disgust. "Why in the world would he do that?"

Grayson laughed even harder. "I dared him that he couldn't put the whole piece in his nose."

"Eww!" Olivia rolled her eyes and turned back to her friends.

Zoey wrinkled her nose. "O—M—G! Jackson is so gross!"

Emily twisted in her seat. "What did he do now? I couldn't hear Grayson."

"Apparently, Grayson dared him to put an entire piece of ham up his nose, and the goofball did it!" Zoey said.

Tommi's eyes widened. "You mean he put a whole slice of ham in his nose?"

Zoey frowned. "No, he was only able to fit half a slice up there. But still, that is so nasty."

The girls all agreed that boys could be so gross, then packed up their things to head back to class.

The afternoon went by quickly, and Zoey noticed that Josh didn't talk to her the way he normally did during class. She wasn't sure why things felt different—she didn't like Josh, at least not like that, and she didn't think that he liked her. *Ugh! Why did Trudy have to open her big, fat mouth?*

When Zoey got home from school, she couldn't wait to tell Jasmine about her day. She dropped her backpack at the bottom of the stairs, then hurried to the kitchen to update Jasmine on today's events.

"JASMINE! Where are you?

"In here!" Jasmine yelled.

Letting out an exaggerated sigh, Zoey entered the family room. Jasmine had already changed out of her school clothes and wore a pair of joggers and a t-shirt. She sat on the couch, eating popcorn and watching an episode of *Absolute Drama.*

"When did you get home?" Zoey asked.

"I got sick at school and mom had to come and pick me up right before lunch," Jasmine replied casually, munching on a mouthful of popcorn. She moved over on the sofa to make room for Zoey.

Zoey sat beside her. "Well, you didn't seem sick this morning."

Jasmine gave her a smirk. "I wasn't feeling well this morning, and I thought I would start to feel better, but I didn't. The nurse called mom because I had a fever, Miss Nosey Pants. So, what's up?"

"Today at school, Trudy blurted out in front of everyone that Josh Hightower is in love with me," Zoey said with a huff.

"Why in the world would she say that?"

"Who knows?" Zoey crossed her arms and sunk into the sofa. "Well, Mrs. P had us break into groups to do a science experiment called *Elephant Toothpaste.*"

Zoey brought her up to speed on how the experiment worked. "And when it was time to clean up, I picked up the tray to put the supplies away, and Trudy snatched the tray right out of my hand and spilled blue food coloring on my sweater! Luckily Mrs. P was able to get the stain out. And then when Josh told her that it was her fault that my sweater got stained, she told him to shut up because everyone knows that he's in love with me."

Jasmine munched another handful of popcorn. "You can't let people treat you any kind of way, Zo. I would have snatched the tray back from her."

Zoey looked at her sister as if she'd lost her mind. "I'm not trying to start a fight."

"I'm not saying that, but you have to stand up for yourself."

"Oh, I'm not scared of her!"

"Well good. Is she bigger than you?" Jasmine asked.

"She's bigger than everyone in class, even the boys. And she's sort of—pudgy."

"Um hmm, and I bet she uses her size to try to intimidate people too." Jasmine said, shaking her head. "You are gonna have to deal with her sooner or later, Zo." She poked Zoey's arm playfully. "So, what is this about Josh? Do you think he likes you?"

"I don't know. I didn't think so. But after she said it, he ignored me for the rest of the day."

Jasmine gave her a sympathetic look. "I'm sure that everything is fine." She gave Zoey a reassuring smile.

"I hope so." Zoey wanted to believe her sister. "Hey, did you get any more notes from your secret admirer?"

Jasmine's face lit up like a Christmas tree. "No, but I found out who he is." She beamed. "It's this boy named Case who's in my history class."

Zoey sat up, no longer focused on her own drama. "How'd you find out?"

"Aubrey told me he asked her if I had a boy-friend, so I'm pretty sure it's him."

"What's he look like?"

"He's ca-yute!" Jasmine gushed.

"I'm not surprised. The cute boy's always like you!" Zoey chuckled. Jasmine was smart, funny, and very pretty—and always in chill mode.

"Well, I'm gonna grab a quick snack before I start my homework." Zoey got up from the couch and headed into the kitchen.

"See ya later." Jasmine stretched out on the sofa and continued watching her tv show.

Zoey only had to study for her spelling test and do a reading and comprehension worksheet. After she completed her homework, she practiced some of her dance moves for the school talent

show. They were supposed to have another rehearsal that weekend, but since Josh's party was
on Sunday, her mom said she would try to move
it to the next day.

Later that evening, Zoey's mom made her five-
alarm chili for dinner with a three alarm version
for Zoey and her sister.

Once Zoey and her parents settled around the
table to eat, she threw a few crackers in her chili
and asked her mom, "Where's Jasmine?"

"She's upstairs asleep," her mom replied. "She
was still running a fever, so I gave her something
for her temperature and told her to get some rest."

Mr. Lyndon took a heaping bite of his chili,
then swallowed. "Sounds like she may need to
stay home tomorrow."

Mom stirred her steaming chili with a spoon. "I
already told her that I'm going to keep her home
with me."

"Well, I hope she feels better," Zoey said.

"So, what did you do at school today?" Her dad
asked, then wolfed down another spoonful of chili.

"Ugh!" Zoey let out a big sigh.

Her dad just chuckled. "That bad, huh?"

Zoey told them about their cool science experiment, about Trudy snatching the tray from her, and about what she blurted out to the whole class. She also told them that Jackson Smith tried to put an entire piece of ham up his nose but was only able to fit half a slice.

Her mom gave Zoey a questioning look. "Why in the world would he do that?"

"Grayson dared him."

Dad just laughed and shook his head. "Boys will be boys."

"Sounds like I need to have a talk with Mrs. Pennington and Mr. Bradshaw about this Trudy girl!" Her mom stated with concern. "This is the same girl who hit you in the face with the ball in gym class. And now, she is intentionally showing aggression towards you. Oh no, we are not having this!" She insisted with a furrowed brow. "Sounds like this little girl doesn't have any home training."

"Rachel, that sounds like a good idea," Zoey's dad replied. "Why don't you set up a meeting and let me know when it is, because I want to attend it with you," he said with a serious tone. "Zoey, we want you to respect your teachers, Mr. Bradshaw, and even your classmates. However, we will not tolerate you being bullied or micro-aggressive behavior."

He had stopped eating and was now resting both elbows on the table, one hand clutched in the other under his chin, his face serious.

"What is micro-aggressive behavior?" she asked him.

"Microaggression is the daily, subtle, intentional, and often unintentional discriminatory behavior directed at a marginalized group of people."

"Huh! What's that?" Zoey asked, with a confused look.

"It's when people treat you differently because of the color of your skin, sex, or your economic background," he said.

"A marginalized group are those that society deems as powerless or impoverished, usually minorities. Mom interjected. "However, I don't think that is the issue in this case," Mom stated matter-of-factly.

"Sounds like we need to get in front of this situation." Her Dad said.

Even though Zoey's parents sometimes volunteered at her school, it was unusual for them to both want to meet with the principal. She knew they were not happy about this Trudy situation. Zoey hoped that Mrs. P wouldn't be mad when her mom called to meet with her.

Zoey's mom wiped her lips with her napkin and turned her attention to Zoey. "Since you and your friends are going to Josh's birthday party on Sunday, I texted the girls' mothers and told them we would move this week's dance rehearsal to Saturday evening at six o'clock. Since Jasmine's school dance starts then, your dad will probably leave around five-thirty to drop her off."

"Oh, that's great!" Zoey replied. "I was wondering if we were gonna have time to rehearse this week."

They finished their meal, then Zoey's dad helped her clean the kitchen since Jasmine wasn't feeling well. Once they were done, Zoey decided to watch a little tv before getting ready for bed.

Chapter 5

Class Comedian

Zoey was looking forward to the weekend ... only two more days to go. Her friends were coming over on Saturday to work on the dance and get ready for the talent show, and she couldn't wait for Josh's party on Sunday. She hoped it wouldn't be awkward.

That morning, Zoey's dad dropped her off at school since Jasmine was at home sick. Mom said she wasn't running a temperature, but she kept her home to get some rest.

In class, Mrs. P wore a super cute pair of navy-blue pants with a gold and white stripe down the side of the leg, a camel-colored blazer, and a pair of gold pumps that matched the stripe on her pants. Zoey thought to herself, *Mrs. P has to be one of the best dressed teachers I've ever had.*

She said her usual good mornings to her friends, but Josh still didn't seem like his normally cheery-self. He did say hello and made eye contact with her, but he didn't smile.

Mrs. P covered their social studies lesson. The students were learning about the forty-six United States presidents. Everyone from George Washington, John Adams, Thomas Jefferson, and James Madison to the more recent ones like George W. Bush, Barack Obama, and of course, the current sitting president, Joe Biden.

Once they finished with the lecture, Mrs. P went right into a reading lesson. Zoey started to nod off as her classmates were reading the different passages of text. The only thing that kept her awake was the clickity-clack of Mrs. P's gold pumps as she walked around the classroom.

Finally, it was time for lunch. Everyone was ready to zonk out from information overload from the morning lessons.

Zoey found her usual table and unpacked her lunch as she waited for her friends to go through the lunch line. Today was pizza day and although Tommi usually packed, she always bought the school lunch on pizza days.

Jackson stopped next to Zoey on his way to his seat. "Hey, Zoey. Can I borrow your hot sauce for my pizza?"

Zoey turned to hand him the bottle. "Sure."

"I'll bring it right back." He took the bottle and headed to his seat.

Emily, Tommi, and Olivia all set their trays down on the table. Olivia was saying something about Grayson and his knock-knock jokes. Zoey caught only the tail end of the conversation and figured she would hear it sooner or later, because Grayson thought he was such a comedian.

"I can't wait for our dance rehearsal on Saturday," Olivia said.

"Yasss! Mrs. Lyndon is going to make sure we are ready for the talent show," Emily replied. She wore one of her signature pink and sparkly outfits.

Tommi swallowed a bite of pizza. "I hope y'all have been practicing the dance moves. I have the

Milly Rock and Billy Bounce down pretty good, but I still need some help with my Moonwalk." She looked at Zoey and reached out her hand. "Can I have some hot sauce?"

"I gave it to Jackson."

The words were barely out of her mouth when Grayson walked over to return the bottle for Jackson.

"Thanks, Zoey!" He said as he handed it back. "You guys wanna hear something funny?" He looked like he was about to burst.

"Sure," the girls replied in unison.

"Knock-knock." He smirked, trying to keep a straight face.

"Who's there?" the girls asked.

"Dishes."

"Dishes who?"

"Dishes the police. Open up and let me in!" He started cracking up as he walked back to his table.

"He's so lame!" Olivia rolled her eyes.

Zoey, Tommi, and Emily giggled.

Zoey shrugged. "He is a bit corny, but the joke was funny."

She handed Tommi her bottle of hot sauce, and Emily added a few drops to her slice.

Olivia got everyone back on topic. "Well, I still need some practice with pretty much all of the dance moves. I'll be ready for the talent show though."

"You'll be fine. We all need a lot more practice," Tommi chimed. She glanced at Zoey. "So how are things with you and Josh?"

Shrugging her shoulders, Zoey answered truthfully. "I'm not sure. He spoke to me this morning, so I guess everything is cool."

"Well, I'm looking forward to his party on Sunday," Emily said. "I heard the place is amazing!"

"I've never been to Sports Fusion, but I am looking forward to going." Zoey took the last bite of her turkey sandwich.

The girls finished up their pizza and cleaned their area to get ready to head back to class. Mrs. P stood in her regular spot by the door and gave them a smile as they passed by. They stopped for a restroom break, then headed back to class.

They stood in the hallway outside the restrooms, the boys were being rowdy and cracking up at Grayson's knock-knock jokes.

"Knock-knock?"

"Who's there?" asked Jackson.

"Anita."

"Anita who?"

"Ah-nita poop." Grayson and the rest of the boys howled with laughter.

"Grayson, if you need to go to the bathroom— now is the time to go," Mrs. P joked from the doorway.

"I'm good," he responded.

Mrs. P gave him a little smile, "Let's go, class." The afternoon flew by and luckily, she didn't give out any homework.

The students packed up to go home, and Mrs. P called out, "See you all tomorrow."

Zoey wondered how Jasmine was doing since she hadn't been feeling well that morning. When she got home, she carried her backpack upstairs to her room to avoid having her mother fuss at her, then peeped into Jasmine's room. But her sister wasn't there. Her bed was made up, so she must be feeling better. Zoey headed downstairs to see if she was in the family room.

Jasmine lay on the sofa and moved her feet so Zoey could plop down on the edge.

"Hey Jazz, how ya feeling?" Zoey asked.

"I feel good! I could have gone to school, but mom wanted to play it safe."

Their mom came in from getting the mail. "Looks like you have a letter." She handed an envelope to Jasmine, then looked at Zoey. "Oh, and by the way, Zoey, your father and I are going to meet with Mr. Bradshaw and Mrs. P on Monday morning."

Zoey nodded, happy that they were taking the issues with Trudy seriously.

Their mom shifted her focus back to Jasmine. "So, who's the letter from?"

Jasmine sat her bowl of popcorn on the table. Smiling from ear to ear, she took the letter from her mother. "It's from Case Morgan." She beamed.

"And who is Case Morgan?" her mom asked with a raised brow.

"He's Jasmine's secret admirer," Zoey gushed. "Or should I say he *was* her secret admirer."

Jasmine's smile grew wider. "Awe, that was so nice of him. He must have put it in the mailbox after school. I wonder how he knows where I live?"

"I think he's a stalker," Zoey teased. She grabbed a handful of popcorn.

"No, he's not!" Jasmine said. "I think it's kind of romantic."

Their mom crossed her arms. "I'm with Zo, that sounds a bit stalkerish. Keep an eye on him." She left the room to take the rest of the mail to the kitchen.

Zoey and Jasmine talked for a while as they watched a couple of their favorite TV shows.

"So, is mom going to let you go to the dance on Saturday?" Zoey asked.

"Yeah. I'm already feeling a lot better."

"You're so lucky! If I were sick, she would totally make me stay home."

"Well, if I was sick, she wouldn't let me go either. But honestly, I feel fine." Jasmine shrugged. "I totally could have gone to school today. Oh, by the way, how are things with you and your boy, Josh?"

"He's not my boy!" Zoey said with a huff. "Things seem okay, I guess. I mean, we still haven't really talked, but he is not ignoring me like he was yesterday."

"I'm sure everything will be back to normal by Monday," Jasmine replied reassuringly. "Oh, mom went out today and picked me up a couple of dresses for the Winter Snow Ball on Saturday."

"Lucky you! You'll need to model them for me." Zoey told her.

"I can show you now. C'mon up." Jasmine motioned for Zoey to follow her upstairs.

"Okay, I'll be up in a sec." Zoey made a pit stop in the kitchen to grab a snack. She settled on some trail mix and picked through the bag to get more pieces of the mini peanut butter cups, then carried her snack upstairs.

She entered Jasmine's room. Jasmine stood in the middle, wearing a pretty, plum-colored, strapless dress.

Zoey admired how beautiful her sister looked in the dress. "Oh, that is pretty! I like that one."

Smiling and slowly twirling around to show off the back, Jasmine stated, "This is option number one."

She pulled it off and put on an ivory-colored, one-shouldered dress with a soft chiffon ruffle on the side. She asked Zoey to help her with the zipper. She was absolutely beaming, which clearly indicated that this was her favorite.

"This is option number two. What do you think?" She sashayed back and forth in her room as if it were a runway on *America's Next Top Model*.

"Oh, Jasmine! That one! You look like a goddess," Zoey gushed.

"This one is my favorite too," Jasmine said with a dreamy look. "I love all the intricate beading and how flowy this fabric is." She gazed at her reflection in the mirror that hung on her closet door.

Zoey wiped off her hands before unzipping the back of the dress so her sister could change out of it. She nibbled on her trail mix while Jasmine showed her the accessories their mom had also picked up to go with both dresses. She modeled the high-heeled shoes and strode back and forth to get comfortable walking in them. Jasmine started wearing high-heels to church over the summer, so even though the heel was three inches, she walked really well in them. Zoey mostly wore flats to church, but she had a pair of kitten heels that she wore on special occasions.

After seeing her sister try on the different options for her dance, Zoey finished her trail mix and decided to practice her Glitz Girls routine for the talent show.

"Girls! Time to eat." Mom yelled up the stairs.

Both girls trotted down the steps to the dinner.

The dinner table was all a buzz as the Lyndon household discussed their day and plans for the weekend. Jasmine's big dance, Zoey's talent show rehearsal, and Josh Hightower's birthday party on Sunday. Dad was looking forward to watching college basketball this weekend. Mom would be busy getting Jasmine ready for her dance and going over new moves with Zoey and her girlfriends.

Since neither of the girls had homework, after dinner, the family settled in to watch a movie.

Chapter 6

Busted

The next morning, Zoey overslept and had to rush to get ready. Luckily, she had laid her clothes out the night before, so it didn't take her long to get dressed. She threw on a pair of black jeans and a gray and white sweatshirt with an owl on it that had two zippers at the bottom. She put on a pair of small, silver hoop earrings and gave herself a quick once over in her mirror, then headed downstairs to the kitchen for breakfast.

Zoey's mom looked at her with pursed lips and shook her head. "You're not going to have enough time to eat breakfast."

Fortunately, her mother had already made toast and there was leftover bacon. Zoey grabbed a piece of buttered toast, a slice of bacon, and an apple to go. She got her coat from the closet and slung her backpack over her shoulder.

"Did Jasmine already leave?" Zoey asked.

"Yes, Zoey, she is probably already at school. Why were you moving so slow this morning?"

"I accidentally went back to sleep after my alarm went off."

"Well, you better hope you're not late. You are cutting it super close this morning, young lady."

Zoey wolfed down her toast and bacon. Carrying her apple in her hand to eat in the car, she and her mom made their way to the jeep and headed to school.

When her mom pulled up in front of the school, Zoey grabbed her backpack and jumped out of the car.

"Bye, Mom. See ya later," she called out, slamming the car door behind her. Hoping she wasn't late, she ran inside the school.

The bell had just finished ringing as she got to Mrs. P's class. She had just made it. She gave a sigh of relief, put her backpack away, and went to her desk.

After Mrs. P took attendance, she stood at the front of the class to get the attention of her students. "Today we have a special treat, after our spelling test this morning. There is a *Fun 4 Kids* assembly, and they are going to talk about fire safety and prevention. So, let's get started." She picked up her spelling book. "The only thing you should have on your desk right now is a pencil and a blank sheet of paper."

Mrs. P had them stand in line after the spelling test and reminded everyone to be on their best behavior. She told them if she caught anyone talking during the assembly, they would lose five minutes of their recess. Zoey was certain that Mrs. P was strict during assemblies because she didn't want her class acting up in front of Mr. Bradshaw, the school Principal.

They walked down to the gymnasium in a single file line, quietly. Mrs. P guided them to the back of the gym and had them sit behind the other fourth grade class. Zoey sat with her legs crossed between Josh and Tommi.

A man in a suit got up in front of the school and began a lecture about fire drills.

"OMG! This is so boring," Zoey whispered to Tommi.

"No kidding. We already know not to play with fire." She let out an exaggerated sigh. "Stop, Drop, and Roll. They've only been telling us this stuff since we were in kindergarten," she said, rolling her eyes.

Zoey changed the subject. "I'm looking forward to laser tag this weekend."

"Me too. I think it's going to be a lot of fun." Tommi said.

Zoey was ready to say something else but saw Mrs. P's harsh gaze which caused her to stop in her tracks. She faced forward and started to pay attention because she didn't want to get in trouble. Tommi snickered under her breath. Zoey listened to the rest of the message about the importance of smoke detectors in the home and how you should regularly check them and replace the batteries at least once a year. After the speaker told them they should never play with matches or lighters, there was a short Q & A session and finally the boring assembly was over.

Once they returned to class, Mrs. P asked everyone to take out their math books. "Okay everybody, please turn to—"

"WHO IN THE HECK TOOK MY NINTENDO!" Josh shouted angrily.

Mrs. P walked to Josh's desk with a worried look. "Are you sure your game is missing?"

"Yes, Mrs. P. I put it in my desk this morning before we had our spelling test, and I saw it before we went to the assembly."

Zoey felt bad for Josh. She could tell he was really ticked off because his nostrils kept flaring and he wouldn't sit down. Looks like the sticky finger bandit had struck again.

Mrs. P crossed her arms. "Jackson, go to the office and see if Mr. Bradshaw is available. Tell him I need him to come to our classroom." She turned to the class with a frown. "Now, I don't know who took Josh's Nintendo, but this is the time to speak up."

The class was so quiet you could hear a pin drop. Everyone looked around the room to see who was going to fess up, but no one said a word. Zoey could tell that Mrs. P was mad because she had never called for Mr. Bradshaw before. *Maybe now we will find out who has been stealing our stuff.* She wondered if she would get her pencils back.

After a few minutes, Jackson came back with Mr. Bradshaw. Mrs. P told him what had been happening to the student's things in the classroom. She told him that Josh's Nintendo Switch had gone missing sometime during the assembly.

Mr. Bradshaw was tall and had a very deep voice—he was the type of Principal who was not to be played with.

He looked around the room with an intense gaze. "I don't know who has Josh's Nintendo, but I know for a fact that he is extremely distraught that it's missing! If you have it or know who does, speak up now" he cautioned with a stern tone.

The class was dead silent and again, no one spoke up.

"Okay, have it your way." Mr. Bradshaw told everyone to get their backpacks and bring them to their desks. He then walked to each student and asked them to empty their bags.

Josh sat in his seat, anxiously tapping his fingers on his desktop. Zoey was sure he hoped Mr. Bradshaw would find the culprit.

Mr. Bradshaw had gone through half of the class and still hadn't found the Nintendo when he reached Jackson. Jackson emptied his backpack and picked his Nintendo out of the pile. He held it up nervously and said, "Uh...this is mine."

Mrs. P nodded. "That belongs to him, Mr. Bradshaw. He brings it to school every day."

When Trudy Jacobs dumped her backpack onto her desk, Josh's Nintendo tumbled out.

Suddenly, a chorus of "Oh's" filled the room from the other students.

Mr. Bradshaw picked up the Nintendo and asked Trudy, "Is this yours?"

Trudy dropped her head and slowly shook it no.

Mrs. P walked to Trudy's desk, shaking her head the way that disappointed teachers do. "Trudy, why did you take Josh's game? Those things are very expensive, and you knew he would be upset."

Trudy stared at her feet.

Mrs. P took the game from Mr. Bradshaw and paused, staring at the pile. She picked up a half-used butterfly eraser and a light blue pencil nub that said *Be Happy*. "Did you take these from Zoey and Olivia?"

Trudy looked as if she were on the verge of tears.

"Trudy, I need you to come with me," Mr. Bradshaw commanded.

She rose from her desk, her head still hung low, and followed him out the door.

Mrs. P handed Josh his Nintendo and told him to put it inside his desk. She asked Olivia and Zoey if they wanted their items back, and both girls said no. Mrs. P put them in her desk drawer, and she resumed class.

"Please pull out your math books and turn to chapter eighteen."

Class was back on track, but it was hard for everyone to focus after all the excitement. Zoey couldn't believe that Trudy had taken Josh's Nintendo—and that the girl had stashed her pencil and Olivia's eraser in her backpack. After watching her take the walk of shame to Mr. Bradshaw's office, she kind of felt bad for her. Zoey wasn't sure why, because she had no business stealing their stuff.

They were in the middle of going over their math problems when the classroom phone rang. It was the school secretary calling, requesting that Josh come to Principal Bradshaw's office immediately.

Jackson looked at Josh, who shrugged his shoulders and got up to leave.

Later that afternoon, the lunch table was buzzing with chatter about the sticky finger bandit—also known as Trudy Jacobs.

"OMG! Can you believe that Trudy took Josh's Nintendo?" Blurted Emily as she sat down with her lunch tray.

"I can't believe Principal Bradshaw had everyone empty out their backpacks," Tommi said.

"It's a good thing he did, otherwise Josh wouldn't have got his game back." Zoey put a few drops of hot sauce on her turkey and cheese sandwich.

"Well at least we know who was taking all of our stuff," said Olivia. "Can you believe that she still had my eraser and your pencil, Zoey? If I would have taken them, I wouldn't have kept them in my backpack." She shook her head and rolled her eyes, then took a bite of her cheese pizza.

Josh and Jackson sat down across from the girls. Normally they sit with the other boys at the end of the table, but every now and then they liked to join Zoey and her squad.

"Wassup!" Josh greeted the girls with a slight head nod.

"Hey Zoey, can I get some of your hot sauce?" Jackson asked.

"Sure, here you go." She handed him the bottle. Zoey remembered that he liked hot sauce on his pizza.

After sprinkling a few drops on his slice, he handed the bottle back to Zoey. He directed his gaze to Josh. "So, why'd you get called down to Mr. Bradshaw's office?"

"Yeah, what happened?" Zoey asked.

Josh had just taken another bite of his pizza and held up his index finger before answering. "Mr. Bradshaw made Trudy apologize to me."

"Did she?" Tommi questioned skeptically.

"Yeah, she did. I'm not sure if she meant it or not, but she did say she was sorry. I actually feel pretty bad for her." Josh took another bite of pizza.

The girls looked at him like he had lost his mind,

then Olivia blurted, "Why in the world would you feel sorry for her? She's so mean!"

Josh leaned in and spoke in a hushed tone. "She's been having a lot of problems at home, and she had to go live with her Aunt. I could tell she had been crying when I got to Mr. Bradshaw's office."

Everyone processed the news and seemed a little more sympathetic to Trudy's situation. Zoey knew how important her family was to her and couldn't imagine having to leave home to live someplace else. This didn't excuse her stealing, but Zoey understood a little better about why she could be so mean.

Emily changed the subject and started to talk about the talent show. The girls were looking forward to their dance practice this weekend and showing Mrs. Lyndon all of their hard work.

Looking at Josh and Jackson, Olivia asked, "So are you guys going to be in the talent show?"

Jackson smiled and shook his head. "Yeah! We are going to rap."

"Yup!" Josh said.

"Wow! That should be fun. I had no idea you were a rapper," Zoey said with surprise.

"I wouldn't say that I'm a rapper, but I can spit a few rhymes," Josh replied.

Jackson grinned. "Nah, don't let him fool you. Josh got mad skills with the rhymes."

Lunch was just about over when Mrs. P entered the cafeteria and stood by the door. Today she wore a kelly-green dress with a thin, navy-blue belt and a cute sweater (kind of like the ones Zoey's mom always wore). She waved her hand, letting her class know it was time to go.

The afternoon flew by. Mrs. P reviewed a social studies lesson and showed a documentary about Agriculture in the Midwestern Region on the class-room TV. She let everyone snack on popcorn while they watched it.

When the bell rang, Zoey's said bye to her friends as they headed to the bus line. By the time she got to the car-rider line, her mom was already waiting for her. Zoey threw her backpack in the back seat, and then jumped in the front.

"Hey, Mom," she said cheerfully as she slammed the car door shut.

"I see someone's in a good mood." Her mom put

the car in gear and drove away from the school. "How was your day, kiddo?"

"Oh my God! Mom, you are not gonna believe what happened today!"

Smiling at how animated her daughter's face was, she responded, "My goodness! What happened?"

"So, you know how we suspected that someone in our class was the sticky finger bandit?" Zoey replied. "Well, today we found out who it was because they stole Josh's Nintendo Switch."

Her mom turned to her with a surprised look. "Whaaaat?"

Zoey gave her a quick rundown of the classroom drama. She couldn't wait to tell Jasmine when she got home.

After a few minutes of chatting about Zoey's day, her mom pulled the car into their driveway and parked. Zoey jumped out and grabbed her backpack, then ran inside.

"Hey Jasmine! Where are you?" She dropped her backpack by the stairs and found Jasmine in her usual spot in the kitchen having her after-school snack.

"I'm right here." Jasmine paused from taking the last bite of the pepperoni pizza bagel in her hand. "What's up?"

Zoey walked to the table with her hand on her hip. "You are not going to believe what happened today at school!"

Jasmine held her pizza bagel in midair as Zoey told her about the day's events.

"So, you know how we had the sticky finger bandit in our classroom, stealing everybody's stuff? Well, today when we got back from our school assembly, someone stole Josh's Nintendo Switch. When Mrs. P asked if anyone had seen it, no one answered."

"Of course, no one saw anything." Jasmine set her bagel down on the plate and leaned in, placing her elbows on the table.

"Mrs. P was so mad she sent for Mr. Bradshaw, our Principal. When Mr. Bradshaw got to our class, he made everyone get their backpacks and take out the contents as he walked by."

Jasmine leaned in and urged her to continue.

"And when Trudy Jacobs had to empty her backpack—there it was! She had taken Josh's Nintendo!

And get this—Mrs. P found my *Be Happy* pencil and Olivia's eraser in her pile of stuff."

"Wow! So, what happened to her?"

"Well, she was trying to act all tough like always, but you could tell she was scared. She had to go to Mr. Bradshaw's office."

"That is craaaazy! I can't believe she took your boy's Nintendo. I bet he was ticked off." Jasmine shook her head in disbelief, then finished eating her pizza bagels.

"Oh my God! He was so mad! He ended up getting called down to the principal's office too."

Confused, Jasmine asked, "Why in the world did he have to go to the office?"

"Because Mr. Bradshaw made Trudy apologize to him. Josh said she had been crying and apparently has a lot of stuff going on at home. She had to go live with her aunt."

"Awe man, that is messed up. But that is not a reason for her to be acting a fool and stealing everyone's stuff."

"I know, but I kind of feel bad for her. You know, her having to move out of her home and in with her aunt."

"Nah. Don't feel bad for her, Zo. There are a lot of people that have to deal with tough situations, but they are not out here trying to become petty criminals," Jasmine replied. "I could empathize with her having to move in with her auntie, because that must really be hard. But that is still no excuse to hurt other people by taking what doesn't belong to her." She paused and tilted her head. "So, isn't she the same girl that hit you in the face with the ball?"

"Yeah, that's her."

"And she didn't even have the decency to apologize." Jasmine sighed. "Nah, Zo, don't feel sorry for that girl."

Zoey walked to the counter and put a few pizza bagels on a plate and into the microwave, then sat at the table across from Jasmine.

"Sooo, any more notes from Mr. Case Morgan?" she teased.

"Nope, not today." Jasmine shrugged. "Although he did sit with me and Aubrey today at lunch."

Zoey's eyes lit up. "Ooh!" Then she teased Jasmine as she sang, "Jasmin and Case sitting in a tree ... K-I-S-S-I-N-G."

"I swear Zo, you can be so childish sometimes!" Jasmine got up to put her dirty plate in the sink and headed up the stairs.

"Hey, do you wanna watch an episode of *Absolute Drama* before you get started on your homework?" Zoey yelled out to her.

Jasmine paused, then quickly said, "Sure, but only if you're not going to act immature!" Then she said quickly, "I'll meet you in the family room when you're finished."

After Zoey ate her snack and put her plate and glass in the sink, she went to watch the show with her sister. They ended up watching two episodes and half of a third one before they decided to get started on their homework. Since both girls had plans this weekend, they didn't want to have their homework looming over their heads and decided to get it done early.

Friday nights in the Lyndon household usually meant pizza and a game or some Disney movie that the girls picked out. After Zoey and Jasmine finished their homework, they settled in the living room to watch one of their favorites, *Beauty and the Beast*.

"I'm starting the movie," Jasmine yelled out to their parents, who were in the kitchen.

Their dad entered the room with two pizzas and set them down on the coffee table. "What are we watching tonight, girls?"

The introductory music of the movie began to play just as their mom walked in with her hands filled with napkins, paper plates, and drinks. She set them down next to the pizzas and said, "Take one guess."

Zoey moved over to make room for them on the couch.

Their dad recognized the theme music and muttered, "Ugh ... not again!" He said with a smirk and plopped down onto the worn leather sofa.

Midway through the movie, a distinctive, muffled grinding sound caused the girls and their mom to look at their dad.

"Mooom!" Zoey whined.

Mrs. Lyndon chuckled at how quickly her husband could fall asleep. "Okay, Okay. I'll get him." She got up from her chair and tapped him on his shoulder. "David." She tapped him again. "David! Wake up."

"Huh—what's the matter?" He opened his eyes groggily and looked around.

"Daddy, you fell asleep and were snoring," Jasmine said.

He chuckled out loud. "I'm sorry, girls. I must have been tired."

Their mom put her hands on her hips. "You two go ahead and finish the movie. I'm going to go upstairs with your dad. But first, I'm taking these pizza boxes out to the garage to put them in the recycle bin.

"Okay, Mom," Zoey and Jasmine responded in unison.

Their mother turned to leave, then glanced over her shoulder. "Jasmine, please put our drinks in the kitchen when the movie is over?

"Sure, Mom."

Jasmine and Zoey finished watching the movie and decided to watch a couple more episodes of *Absolute Drama*, including the episode they didn't finish earlier. Afterwards, they carried their paper plates and drinks to the kitchen to throw them away. Jasmine put her parent's unfinished drinks in the refrigerator.

Chapter 7

Jasmin's Big Night

Saturday morning, Zoey went trotting down the stairs to the smell of her dad's home-cooked breakfast. She entered the kitchen and to her delight, pancakes, eggs, sausage, and hash browns had already been placed on the table.

Mrs. Lyndon walked into the room behind her. "Umm—something sure does smell good." She went to the kettle to make a cup of rose and vanilla tea.

"Good morning," the girls greeted their parents in unison and took their seats.

"Morning, girls." Their father winked as he brought the syrup and ketchup over to the table.

"Good morning," Mom replied, as she poured hot water from the kettle into her cup. "Jasmine, we're going to head out after we eat. Your appointment is at ten-thirty this morning."

Jasmine nodded and said okay. She hummed as she enjoyed the pancakes and syrupy sweetness she had drizzled all over them. "Daddy, you always make the best pancakes."

"Yeah, I love when you make your famous pancakes," Zoey agreed.

Looking at all of the food on the table, Mrs. Lyndon shook her head. "David, you always cook way too much food. You know the girls aren't going to eat all of this."

He chuckled and sat in his usual chair. "Well at least we won't have to cook tomorrow before church."

She shook her head again and sipped her tea.

After breakfast, Zoey and her father cleaned the kitchen while Jasmine and their mother went to the hair salon. Once everything had been put away and the kitchen was tidy, her dad went to see which college teams were playing that day. It didn't really matter who was playing—he just enjoyed watching the game.

Zoey had chores that needed to get done before her friends arrived later for rehearsal. She started with her bedroom, since that was going to take the longest. She was supposed to put away her clean clothes, but she didn't have any room because her drawers were still filled with summer clothing. It was impossible to fit her winter items inside. She finally packed away her summer things in the clear tote her mom had brought up from the basement. Once that was done, her sweaters and shirts fit neatly into her dresser.

Now that she had completed that herculean task, she could finally work on the bathroom that she and Jasmine shared. She wiped down the sink and made sure to put the old towels in the hamper. The toilet paper roll was practically empty, so she went to get another from the linen closet.

Just then, the garage door opened with a grinding noise. *That must be Mom and Jasmine* she thought to herself. *I'll run down to see them in a minute.* She wanted to finish the bathroom first.

When she opened the linen closet, the Angel Soft tissue they normally used wasn't there. In its place sat some generic tissue. *Hmm, Mom must be trying out something new.* She ripped open the package and pulled out a couple rolls to put in their bathroom, then stopped in her tracks.

She unrolled a couple of sheets and was absolutely appalled. "Ugh! Who in the heck bought one-ply toilet paper?".

Having a pet peeve is not uncommon. In the Lyndon household, Jasmine's pet peeve was that she couldn't stand the noises people make while they are eating. For some reason, that smacking sound went all the way through her. Their father didn't like it when people wouldn't look him in the eye when they were talking, and their mother absolutely hated it when people constantly said *um* when they talked. It drove her crazy. Apparently, one-ply toilet tissue was the thing that annoyed Zoey to no end. She clearly had no problem using sub-standard tissue paper at school but was grateful they had the good stuff at home.

Marching downstairs and holding the single ply roll of one thousand sheets of the generic tissue as if it was a culprit of some committed crime, she strode into the kitchen, where her family was already gathered.

Her mother was telling her husband something about a road closure near Interstate seventy when Zoey rudely interrupted their conversation. "MOM! Why did you buy this toilet paper?" She huffed. "Did you know that it is only one-ply?" She thrust the tissue forward like it was a rotten egg.

Zoey's mother and father looked at one another with confusion and then at Zoey as if she had lost her mind.

"Little girl, just who do you think you are talking to?" Her mother snapped in her cool and calm voice. "Number one—I know that you know better than to address your father or me in that disrespectful tone. Number two—I didn't buy the toilet paper. Your father did."

"You owe your mother an apology," her dad said in his scolding voice, the one he only used when he was disappointed with something the girls did.

Immediately feeling ashamed about how she acted, Zoey dropped her head. "Sorry, Mommy."

Jasmine collected her things and quietly exited the kitchen. Zoey didn't blame her one bit. Zoey had messed up and would rather be anywhere but here right now.

ZOEY LYNDON AND THE STICKY FINGER BANDIT

"As a matter of fact, I want you to march yourself back up those stairs and try coming down again. This time, like you've got some sense," her father demanded.

Zoey returned up the steps only to walk down them again.

"Now, is there something that you wanted to ask?" her mother said in her don't-play-with-me voice.

Zoey softened her tone and respectfully answered, "Yes. I wanted to know if you knew that this new toilet paper is only one-ply? I think maybe you bought the wrong toilet paper."

Dad crossed his arm. "I bought it intentionally. You and your sister go through so much toilet paper that I purchased this because it has a lot more sheets on each roll."

"Seriously, Daddy!" Zoey replied. "This tissue paper is hard like the paper we use at school. I hate it because it isn't soft. Plus, I don't want my friends to think that we're poor when they come over and have to use the bathroom."

Shaking his head in disbelief. "I didn't realize that switching toilet paper was going to be such a big deal. And no one is going to think that we are poor because of the paper that we have in the bathroom!"

Mom spoke up. "Yeah, Zo, your friends can care less about stuff like that. But babe, that tissue is a bit harsh. I think it'll be okay if we just continue to get the normal stuff."

Throwing his hands up in surrender while simultaneously rolling his eyes, he said, "You guys are too spoiled. Fine! I won't purchase this tissue anymore, but we are going to use it until it is gone."

Later that evening as Mrs. Lyndon helped Jasmine put the final touches on her hair and make-up, Zoey and her father waited anxiously for her to come downstairs.

Her father beamed when Jasmine entered the room. Zoey could tell his heart was swelling with pride because it took him a moment to find his words.

"You look absolutely beautiful!"

"Thank you, Daddy. Do you like my dress? Mom picked it out for me." Jasmine twirled around.

Giving a big thumbs up, he nodded. "Mom did good!" He pulled out his camera from the bag on the side table and adjusted the lens. "Now, give me a big smile!"

Zoey had already seen her in the dress but with her hair and make-up complete, she looked like she could be in high school. "You look great, Sis!"

"Thanks, Zo." Jasmine smiled.

Her father snapped a few pictures to capture the moment, despite Jasmine complaining that he always took fifty million pictures.

Finally, Mom interrupted. "David, you two should get going, especially since you still have to pick up Aubrey."

Jasmine put on the ivory-colored wool cape her mom had picked up for her, and she looked like a vision. Zoey knew Jasmine didn't want to wear the big puffy coat she usually wore to school.

"Oh, that looks nice." Mom assured her as she adjusted the cape. "You look like a snow princess."

"Thanks, Mom."

She and her dad waved goodbye as they started to leave.

"Have a good time!" Mom called out as Mr. Lyndon pulled the door closed behind them. She turned to Zoey and pointed towards the basement. "Zoey, I'm going to go set up the music. Your friends should be here shortly."

At six o'clock on the dot, the girls all showed up for dance rehearsal. Mrs. Lyndon told the other moms what time to pick the girls up.

They didn't waste any time getting started. Mrs. Lyndon set up a camera to record the practice so the girls could watch it later.

"Alright, girls. Let's do a quick review, and then we'll put it all together. I'm going to record the routine for you, so that you can work on it at home."

After she cranked up the music, they got started.

Surprisingly, it looked like everyone had practiced, and they were ready to move on. They went over a few more dance steps and once they seemed to grasp those moves, Mrs. Lyndon showed them what the entire routine would look like. The girls watched and tried to memorize it as they bobbed their heads to the beat of the music.

"Oh my God! We are totally going to come in first place in the talent show," Olivia said.

Everyone gave Zoey's mom a round of applause. They were eager to get started practicing the routine.

"Five, six, seven, eight—slide to the right, jump-step, wave the body, open, dip and get that money money." There was a specific dance move associated with each instruction. "Girls', make sure you watch your facial expressions when you are practicing at home. It's important that you keep your face relaxed."

The girls continued to practice the moves until Zoey's mom was sure that they had the steps down.

"Mom, do you mind if we cut our practice a little short? I think we need a break." Zoey asked.

Since they hadn't taken a break yet, her mom agreed to wrap the practice up early. For the remaining twenty minutes, they went upstairs to the kitchen to raid the refrigerator for snacks.

Zoey's mom gave each girl a thumb drive that had a recording of their routine before they left with their parents.

Shortly after the girls' parents picked them up, Aubrey's father, Mr. Davidson, dropped Jasmine off at home. Her parents were in the kitchen enjoying a bowl of ice cream, and Zoey had gone upstairs to shower. Jasmine flung her cape over the back of the sofa in the living room and kicked off her heels.

She entered the kitchen, looking excited. "Ugh! My feet are killing me." She sat at the table with her parents.

"How was the dance?" Mom asked.

"It was fun! Everyone loved my dress. I think I have a blister on my heel from my shoe."

"Oh, no! Let me see." Her mom set her bowl on the table and leaned down to take a closer look. "Yeah, that's what it looks like," she confirmed. "Let's see how it feels tomorrow."

"I thought you and Aubrey were going to hang out after the dance?" Dad asked, then took another bite of his butter pecan ice cream.

"Oh, we decided to hang out here instead. She just went home to change first."

"Tell us about the dance!" Mom asked.

Jasmine leaned in and rested her elbows on the table. "Well, I already told you that everyone liked my dress. Two other girls wore the same one as Aubrey, and so they all took a picture and called themselves Charlie's Angels." She giggled.

"Did you dance?"

She nodded excitedly. "Yes, Mom. All of the girls danced together on a lot of songs." She dropped her head just a smidge. "Case asked me to dance, and so I danced with him twice."

Dad looked confused. "Who is Case?"

"Daddy, he's just some boy at school that likes me."

Her mom pursed her lips. "What about Noah? You haven't mentioned him."

"Well, I still like Noah. He is really nice, but he has a lot of older girls always hanging on him. I don't want to be just another girl. You know?"

Although Jasmine's father didn't say a word, the smile on his face spoke volumes. He must have been happy to see that his daughter had some sense.

She continued, "I did get a chance to talk to him for a little bit tonight, but I think we will just stay friends." She stood up to go to her room and change before Aubrey came back.

"Sounds good to me, kiddo." Her dad got up to put his bowl in the dishwasher.

"Where's Zoey?" Jasmine asked.

"Taking a shower," her mom replied, then took the last bite of her mint chocolate chip ice cream.

Jasmine went and changed into a sweatshirt and shorts. The doorbell rang, and she ran downstairs to bring Aubrey up to her room so they could talk about the dance. Although she told her mom and dad that she had danced with Case, she conveniently left out that both dances were slow and he had asked her to be his girlfriend. She had told him that she needed some time to think about it and would give him an answer on Monday.

Jasmine's mother answered the door—and chatted with Mr. Davidson. Jasmine whisked Aubrey away to discuss a pressing matter.

Wasting no time, Jasmine closed her bedroom door and turned to her friend. "Okay! What should I do?"

Aubrey chuckled and sat on Jasmine's bed. "Well, what do you want to do?"

"Ugh! I don't know. That's the problem." Jasmine paced the room and let out a big sigh.

"Well, Case is really nice. And a lot of girls think he's cute."

Jasmine agreed with Aubrey on both points. She did still like Noah, but she was beginning to realize that he was a little too mature for her. She also didn't like that half the girls at school fawned all over him.

She tapped her chin, thinking. "I agree. Case is cute and really sweet. It was so thoughtful of him to give me that card the other day when I was sick."

"Uh, I'm pretty sure he only did that because he likes you. I mean, I've known him all my life and he has never given me a get-well card."

Jasmine burst out laughing. "I see your point."

"You two looked really cute when you were dancing," Aubrey said.

"Seriously! Really? I was so nervous. I was hoping that I didn't look like a blooming idiot." Jasmine giggled. "When he asked me to dance, my heart was pounding so loud I was hoping he couldn't hear it. And he smelled sooo good!"

Aubrey nodded her head. "I know what you mean! When Miles asked me to dance, I almost wanted to say no. But then I saw you walk out on the dance floor with Case, so I said okay."

"Well at least that's over now," Jasmine joked. "We can both cross off *slow dancing with a boy* from our to-do list."

Both girls cracked up laughing.

"Oh, and by the way, when you and Case were on your second slow dance, Noah came over to ask me who you were dancing with."

"Really?" Jasmine gave a little smirk. "I wonder why he asked."

"I think he likes you, but I told him that you like Case. Plus, he is such a flirt. He knows those silly girls will do anything for him," Aubrey said in exasperation.

Jasmine dropped her head slightly and tried to maintain her composure. She and Noah liked one another, but she had accepted the fact that he was too old for her—at least right now, anyway. And Aubrey didn't need to know that Jasmine liked her brother, especially since she had already decided to just be friends.

The girls continued to talk about the dance. The couples, who was the best dressed boy and girl, and the drama. Jasmine decided she didn't want to be Case's girlfriend, but she would like to get to know him better. Aubrey agreed and thought that was the smart thing to do.

Chapter 8

The Confrontation

The next morning after the Lyndons got home from church, Zoey quickly changed her clothes. They had stopped at one of their favorite local restaurants to have brunch before heading home. Zoey had been looking forward to Josh's birthday party, plus it would be her first time playing laser tag. Fortunately, her mother had picked up a Nintendo gift card for Josh that she put into a gift bag with a birthday card.

Zoey arrived at Sports Fusion promptly at one o'clock. After heading inside with her mom, she waved and took off towards to her friends. "See ya."

"Have a good time," her mom replied, but Zoey wasn't really listening... Mrs. Lyndon introduced herself to Josh's parents and told them she would be back at a quarter to three to pick up her daughter.

Zoey set her gift bag on the table with all the other birthday presents for Josh. She and her friends went to get their laser equipment and were off. When they got inside, it was dark and hard to see until her eyes adjusted. They were having a blast, running around tagging one another with their laser beams and trying to hide. The boys acted like they were doing military tactical training, the way that they were hiding and crawling on the floor as if they were invisible. Finally, a loud buzzer went off, indicating that it was time for birthday cake. The kids dropped off their gear and got ready to leave the laser tag room.

"That was so much fun!" Jackson said as he slapped Josh on his shoulder.

Zoey stood with her girls in the hallway, and Josh gave her a slight wave and thanked them all for coming.

"Thank you for inviting us, this was so much fun," Zoey replied.

As they were walking over to the meeting room to have cake, Josh asked Zoey, "Can I talk to you for a minute?"

"Sure," Zoey hung back behind her friends to walk with him.

"I know I was acting weird the other day when Trudy blurted out that I was in love with you. I don't care what she says, because it's not true." He glanced at Zoey nervously. "I mean, you already know that I like you but, you know—just as a friend."

Zoey smiled, relieved to hear that things were still good between them. He was definitely one of her best friends. "I was a little embarrassed, but I'm glad we are still good."

"For sure. We're cool." He smiled, giving her a slight nudge.

"So, I see that you invited Trudy today. I didn't see that one coming."

His smile quickly left his face. "My mom made me invite her, she said it wouldn't be nice to invite the entire class and exclude her."

Zoey shrugged her shoulders, acknowledging she understood, and went to catch up to her friends.

The girls found their seats around the table, and just as Emily sat down, Trudy snatched the chair out from under her. "This is my seat."

Emily grabbed for the table to try to keep from falling, but still hit the floor with a thud. She looked up at her friends, mad and embarrassed. Zoey instinctively stood and yanked the chair from Trudy as hard as she could.

"SERIOUSLY! I swear ... you are so mean!" Zoey fumed, still gripping the chair.

Trudy's eyes widened in shock—obviously surprised that Zoey was challenging her. She stepped forward menacingly. "I said," she leaned over Zoey and scowled in an attempt to intimidate her, "THIS IS MY SEAT!"

Just then, Tommi and Olivia flanked both sides of Zoey to show that they had her back. Zoey puffed out her chest and stood as tall as she could and looked Trudy dead in her eye. She commanded as forcefully as she could, "No! It is not! And I am sick and tired of your bad attitude and always trying to bully everyone."

Mrs. Hightower came over to where the girls were standing, with Josh trailing behind her. "What seems to be the problem, girls?"

Tommi spoke up first. "We were all sitting down for cake and ice cream when Trudy pulled Emily's chair out from under her and made her fall. She's always trying to bully someone."

Trudy rolled her eyes at Tommi. Mrs. Hightower remained calm and looked at Trudy. "Was Emily sitting in the chair first?"

"No!" Trudy said with a huff.

"She was too, Trudy Jacobs, and you know it!" Zoey snapped.

"Trudy dear, there is an empty seat next to me, how about you come up front and sit with me?" Mrs. Hightower diffused the situation and got the birthday party back on track. Trudy followed her to the front of the table.

"Emily, are you okay?" Zoey asked.

"Yeah, I'm fine." Emily shook her head. "I can't stand her!"

"Oh my God! Zoey, you really stood up to her. I was surprised that you got in her face the way you did," Olivia said.

"I surprised myself." Zoey chuckled. "I was just so fed up with Trudy being mean *all the time*! I just couldn't take it anymore."

Tommi added her two cents. "Well, I think she knows now that you are not scared of her." She boasted and gave her friend a congratulatory pat on the back.

The kids watched Josh open his birthday gifts and enjoyed cake and ice cream cups. Josh thanked everyone for coming.

Parents began to come into the room to pick up their kids. Mrs. Lyndon was talking to Tommi's dad and Emily's parents when the girls walked up to them. Tommi's dad said he was taking Tommi and Olivia home since the girls lived next door to one another. The parents talked briefly about how the dance routine was coming and the upcoming school talent show. Finally, Zoey's mom thanked Josh's parents for inviting her daughter, and Zoey waved goodbye to her friends.

On the ride home, Zoey's mom asked, "So, did you have fun?"

"Yeah. I had a lot of fun, and I think Jasmine would totally like this place. They even had a rock-climbing wall."

"Oh, really?"

"Yes ma'am. We didn't get to climb it, but it looked like fun. Laser tag was awesome, but it was really crowded."

Mrs. Lyndon looked over and smiled at her daughter. "Well, I'm glad you had a good time."

Zoey frowned. "I had a great time until mean ole Trudy tried to bully us again."

"What happened?"

Zoey filled her in about Trudy pulling the chair out from under Emily and how she confronted her about it. She also explained that Mrs. Hightower diffused the situation.

"I'm glad that you stood up for your friend and for yourself. If you don't stand up to bullies, they will keep making your life miserable," her mom replied. "I don't know what this little girl's problem is, but I am glad that we have a meeting with Mrs. P and Mr. Bradshaw in the morning."

When they got home, the evening flew by. After dinner, Zoey hung out with her sister in the living room. She hadn't had a chance to really talk to her about the dance, and she wanted to tell her about Josh's party. Zoey told her, "Josh and I finally had an opportunity to talk, and everything is fine now."

"I knew everything was going to work out, Zo."

Zoey grinned. "Mom said that she and dad are meeting with Mrs. P and the principal tomorrow about Trudy."

"Well, good! Trudy is a bully. It sounds like she has some issues, but she can't take them out on other people and expect that to fly."

The girls decided to watch a little TV before finally getting ready for school tomorrow.

Chapter 9

No More Drama

At lunch the next day, Zoey sat at her usual table, waiting for her friends. The boys were at the end of it, talking about how much fun they had at laser tag. Grayson told more of his corny knock-knock jokes. Trudy sat alone at another table and didn't seem like her usual obnoxious self, at least not towards Zoey and her crew. She wondered what that was about, but her thoughts were interrupted when her friends arrived, complaining about the school lunch.

"I swear—I'm going to have to start packing my lunch because the selection is terrible!" Olivia said, setting her tray onto the table.

"Seriously! I know. I almost packed this morning too," Tommi quickly added.

The lunch staff were serving some disgusting turkey and gravy with fake mashed potatoes. The girls all chose peanut butter and jelly sandwiches, which the school offered every day in the event a student didn't want to eat the normal lunch or forgot their lunch money.

Tommi lifted her PB & J to her mouth and asked, "So how's everybody feeling about the dance routine?" then took a bite.

Emily's face lit up and was animated with excitement. "Oh my gosh! I think I'm getting it! I mean, I still need to practice, but I think I'm doing pretty good."

Olivia placed her sandwich on the table. "I'm so glad your mom made us that video, because it is helping a lot."

Tommi and Emily agreed.

"I still need to practice a few of the combinations," Zoey confessed as she nibbled on her pretzels.

Tommi pursed her lips together and teased, "Girl, please! You know your mom is gonna make sure you have all the steps down."

The girls all laughed.

Zoey decided to change the subject. "My mom and dad had a meeting with Mrs. P and Mr. Bradshaw this morning."

"What for?" Emily took a sip of her chocolate milk.

"Yeah, what's up?" asked Tommi and Olivia at once.

"Well, you know how Trudy is always trying to bully everyone?" Zoey asked. "I think my mom was concerned, because her bullying seems to be getting worse."

"I heard she is having some issues at home, but that doesn't give her the right to be mean to everyone," Olivia said.

The girls finished eating their lunch and were listening to some more of Grayson's jokes.

"What did the shark say when he ate the clown fish?" Grayson asked the boys.

They blurted out a few answers.

ZOEY LYNDON AND THE STICKY FINGER BANDIT

"Tastes a little funny to me." Grayson busted out laughing. "Okay, okay," he said, wanting to get in one more joke. "This is the last one, I swear." He flashed a huge grin. "Why did the man put his feet in the oven?" Before anyone could even answer, he said, "He wanted to pop his corns."

All of the boys were cracking up at this point.

Emily giggled at his last joke, then turned back to her friends. "Oh, I meant to tell you, my mom said she can make us all matching jackets for the talent show."

"Oh my gosh! Really? That's awesome," Zoey responded excitedly. The girls were all hyped to have matching outfits to wear for their dance routine.

When they noticed Mrs. P standing at the cafeteria door in a pair of high waist wide leg camel-colored pants with a cream-colored turtleneck and a dark blue, short waist leather jacket, they knew it was time to go back to class. On the way, they stopped for their daily restroom break.

They stood in line, then Tommi said, "Has anyone noticed that sticky fingers Trudy has completely ignored us today?"

Emily placed her hands on her imaginary hips. "Yeah, I've noticed. I was so ready for her today. After yesterday's drama, I've made up my mind that I'm not going to ignore her stank attitude anymore."

"Well, after Zoey stood up to her yesterday, I think she knows that we have had it with her," Olivia added.

Zoey chuckled. "Well, hopefully she knows that all of us are tired of her bad attitude and aren't going to take it anymore."

Zoey had noticed that although Trudy hadn't bothered any of her friends that day, she was her usual mean self with the other kids in class.

That evening at home, the Lyndon family sat down to a dinner of salmon croquettes, seasoned fried potatoes, and green beans. After everybody dished up, Zoey's parents told her about their meeting with Mrs. P and Mr. Bradshaw.

"We informed your Principal about the passive-aggressive behavior that you have had to endure at the hands of your classmate, Trudy Jacobs," her mom said.

"Now, you girls know that we don't like to get involved in the school yard he-said-she-said, but we will always advocate for you when we feel that you are being treated unfairly," her dad pointed out, then took a forkful of seasoned potatoes.

"Apparently, Trudy is having a lot of personal issues at home," Mrs. Lyndon continued. "There seems to be some issues between Trudy and her mother, and she had to be removed from the home. Trudy's been living with her Aunt temporarily. It seems her father left the family, and they have not been able to move forward." She leaned in, resting her elbows on the table with clasped hands.

"Well, that really sucks for Trudy, but it doesn't give her the right to bully everyone around her," Jasmine said.

Her mother looked at her and spoke very softly. "No, it doesn't. However, knowing what she's dealing with at home helps me to understand a little better, why she has been so mean to Zoey and her friends. Being a bully is never okay and I do feel for her, but my responsibility is to always make sure that you are treated fairly."

"Zo, were there any issues today?" her dad asked.

"Nope! We actually noticed that she pretty much ignored all of us today, which was fine with us."

"That's probably because you checked her yesterday." Jasmine snickered.

"Possibly," their dad agreed. "Once a bully knows you're not afraid of them, they will often leave you alone."

They finished up their dinner and as usual, Jasmine and Zoey had clean-up duty. Once they were done, Jasmine went to her mom's office to talk to her.

"What's up, Jazz?" her mom asked, looking up from the article she was writing on her computer.

"Not much." Jasmine plopped down in the chair and propped her feet up on the striped ottoman.

Her mom gave her the signature raised eyebrow, which let Jasmine know she wasn't buying it.

Jasmine chuckled softly. "Case asked me to be his girlfriend."

"Oh, really?" Her mom sounded surprised. "When was this?

"The night of the dance. I told him I would give him an answer today."

"And?"

"And I told him that I like him, but I think we should just hang out and get to know each other."

"Good girl!" Her mom's voice was warm with approval.

"Yeah, he seemed to be okay with it." Jasmine smiled and fidgeted with the fray on the pillow she was holding.

"Hmm, there seems to be something else bothering you."

"No, not really—I mean I kind of liked Noah, but I decided we should just be friends."

Trying to hide her surprise, her mom casually asked, "Noah—as in Aubrey's brother?"

Jasmine nodded yes.

"Oh, well I suppose that is a good thing. I mean, he is a little too old for you."

Since Jasmine agreed with her mother, she couldn't argue her point. Her mother told her that Case seemed like a nice boy, and Jasmine agreed with her once again. They chatted a bit more, before Jasmine decided it was time to let her mother get back to her writing.

Chapter 10

Briar Ridge Talent Show

Over the next few weeks, Zoey and her friends rehearsed their dance routine to the point where their choreographer declared that they had a good shot at winning the talent show. As promised, Emily's mother made the girls matching sequin bomber jackets. They had black, satin sleeves with a black elastic waistband, and the body was made of sequins. Since Emily's favorite color was pink, her jacket was pink sequins, Olivia's was lime green, Tommi's was blue, and Zoey's was purple. The girls had each purchased a pair of black, cropped leggings and black, glittery

Converse sneakers to complete their outfits. The Glitz Girls were ready.

On the day before the talent show, Zoey tried on her dance outfit to see what it looked like all together. Pleased with how it looked, she headed downstairs to show Jasmine.

Case was over at the house again, hanging out with Jasmine. Zoey thought to herself, *he's becoming a permanent fixture here.*

She entered the living room. He was sitting on the sofa with her sister. "Hi, Case."

"Oh, hey, Zoey." He gave her a smile.

"That looks cute!" Jasmine said, gesturing at Zoey's outfit.

"Thanks, Jazz." Zoey grinned and did her version of a model walk.

Jasmine laughed as her sister showed off her dance outfit. "You betta work!" She snapped her fingers and pursed her lips.

Case decided to get in on the action too. "You go, girl!"

Both girls cracked up at his comment, and Zoey headed to the kitchen.

Jazz music played softly as she walked through the entrance. Her mom stood at the counter, chopping asparagus.

"Hey, Mom. Whatcha cooking?"

Lifting her head slightly to acknowledge her daughter, her mom replied, "grilled chicken, baked mac & cheese, and asparagus." She finished stirring in the milk and cheese for the baked mac. "Zoey you look great! Elle really did a great job making the jacket."

"It looks awesome! I didn't even think that I was going to like the sequins, but they are so pretty," Zoey said, running her hand across the purple sequins.

"You girls are going to be hard to beat tomorrow. I don't think they are ready for the Glitz Girls." Her mom gave her a slight head nod and a grin. "Did you show Jasmine your ensemble?"

"Yeah. She likes it too." Zoey grabbed a few of the red globe grapes from the bowl on the counter and threw one into her mouth. "I see Case is here again."

Her mom turned down the music slightly. "Oh, I like Case. He's a nice boy."

"I like him too, but he doesn't have to be here every day."

Mrs. Lyndon chuckled at her daughter's exaggeration. "Now, you know he does not come over every day."

"Well, it sure seems like it." Zoey popped a few more grapes into her mouth. "Who is this singing?"

Her mom placed the pan of baked mac into the oven and started to chop the asparagus. "Ah, this my dear is my man, Mr. John Coltrane, 'Too Young To Go Steady.'"

"I'm going to go change and get my homework out of the way."

"Okay, Zo."

Her mom grooved to the sounds that floated throughout the kitchen. Zoey didn't much care for jazz music, but her parents liked to listen to it from time to time. When they did, Zoey and Jasmine would always take that as their cue to exit the room.

After dinner, the girls watched an episode of *Absolute Drama*.

"So, is Case your boyfriend now?" Zoey teased.

Jasmine gave her sister some major side-eye. "What if he is, Miss Nosey pants?"

"Oh, does that mean yes? I mean, he acts like he is. He's over here almost every day." Zoey smirked.

"I guess you can say that we are dating," Jasmine replied.

"Oh my gosh! I knew it!" Zoey gloated, grinning from ear to ear.

Jasmine changed the subject. "Are you ready for your big day tomorrow?" She grabbed a handful of popcorn.

Zoey's face lit up. "Oh yeah! I can't wait to show everyone our outfits. We are gonna look so good!"

"For sure you are. Emily's mom really hooked you up with those custom jackets."

Zoey ended up watching the end of the episode by herself, because Jasmine was too busy texting Case. Finally, Jasmine went upstairs to her room so they could facetime. Zoey wondered what in the heck they could have to talk about that couldn't wait until tomorrow. She figured this must be what it's like to date a boy. She finished watching her show and decided to head up to her bedroom.

The next day at school, the students were hyped up in anticipation of the talent show taking place later that day. Zoey found it hard to concentrate when Mrs. P was reviewing the homework, but the clickety-clack sound of her high-heeled knee boots snapped her out of her daze. They muddled through a history lesson, a fire drill, a visit to the library, and the afternoon flew by.

The talent show didn't start until six o'clock that evening. Zoey was able to go home, do her homework, and get a quick snack before it was time to head back to school. She dressed in her Glitz Girls costume, and Jasmine leant her a pair of hoops to wear in her ears and put a little cherry blossom lip gloss on her.

Zoey popped her lips together and smiled at her reflection. "I look good!"

Jasmine nodded in agreement. "Okay, Zo. We better get going."

Just then, their mom called out, "Let's go! You don't want to be late."

Zoey jogged down the steps with her sister following. Her mom stood by the door, waiting for them.

Zoey grabbed her coat from the closet. "Where's Daddy?"

Mrs. Lyndon ushered her daughters out the door. "He had to work late—he said he would meet us at school."

Zoey looked worried, "I hope he doesn't miss it!"

Jasmine patted her on her shoulder and assured her he would be there. They drove to the school, parked, and headed into the gymnasium. The students who were participating in the talent show had to report backstage. Zoey's mom and sister followed Zoey there to make sure everything was ready and to double check the music. Once Mrs. Lyndon was certain everything was in order, she and Jasmine went to find their seats.

Mr. Lyndon was already seated by the time they got there.

The show started promptly at six o'clock. Mr. Bradshaw welcomed the audience and asked everyone to silence their cellular devices. The lights dimmed and the first act was introduced. A fifth grade boy opened the show with his acoustic guitar. The second act was a girl who twirled her baton to "Girls Like You" by Maroon 5.

The Glitz Girls were the fourth act to perform, and the girls were super excited. They stood ready in their sparkly sequined jackets, and when their song "Mi Gente" pulsed through the auditorium. They were ready. They executed the dance routine perfectly. Even Olivia's freestyle was amazing! The girls' energy was outstanding, and the audience cheered like crazy.

"Oh my God! They killed it!" Jasmine squealed to her mother. They both got to their feet to give a standing ovation.

Mrs. Lyndon beamed with pride as she clapped enthusiastically. "They sure did!" She took her seat to watch the rest of the show.

There was a total of ten acts in all. Zoey's friends, Josh Hightower and Jackson Smith, were the last to perform. They called themselves the J Squad and performed "God's Plan" by Drake. Josh and Jackson both sang the hook of the song.

They took turns with the verses, and everyone was surprised at how good they were. They had amazing energy, and everyone was rocking and singing along in their seats.

No one was surprised at the end of the talent show when Mr. Bradshaw declared Josh and Jackson the winners. The first place prize were two tickets each to the St. Louis Aquarium. The Glitz Girls came in second place, and won a pizza party and a movie that they would have next week during lunch. The kid with the acoustic guitar came in third place and won a free ice cream Sunday during homeroom.

After the awards, Zoey's mom greeted the girls in the school lobby and gave them each a big hug. "I am so proud of you!"

"I just knew we were going to win!" Emily exclaimed.

Zoey agreed. "We would have taken first place, but Josh and Jackson were really good."

Tommi replied, "Who knew that they could rap? And had the nerve to be good on top of that!"

They were all happy for their friends because they deserved to win. And besides, second place was not too shabby.

———

That evening at home, Zoey was still pretty excited and didn't want to get ready for bed yet. She decided to go talk to Jasmine.

"Hey, Jazz. Whatcha doing?" Zoey asked as she tapped on the door. It wasn't closed all the way, so she walked in.

Jasmine sat on her bed with her phone. "Nothing at the moment. Wassup?"

"Not much, I'm still a little hyped about the talent show."

"You and your girls killed it! Plus, y'all had the best outfits too."

Jasmine stared at her phone, texting while she talked.

"Is that Aubrey or your boyfriend?" Zoey teased.

"It's Case, my boyfriend." Jasmine smirked.

"Wait—what?" Zoey asked.

Jasmine's giggles were all the confirmation Zoey needed. Both girls busted out laughing.

"When did this happen?" Zoey asked curiously.

"Today. Case is so nice, and I really like talking to him. He makes me laugh, and he is super cute."

The girls talked a little while longer before Jasmine finally kicked Zoey out of her room because Case had just facetimed her.

As Zoey got ready to take a shower and get her clothes ready for tomorrow, she noticed how happy her sister seemed now that she had a boyfriend. Boys always seemed to like her sister, and Zoey couldn't help but wonder if anyone would ever like her? Not that she was ready for a boyfriend, but she hoped that when she was, they would come as easy for her as they did for Jasmine. But that was a problem for another day.

The End

TEACHER'S GUIDE

Available at
everythingmicheal.com

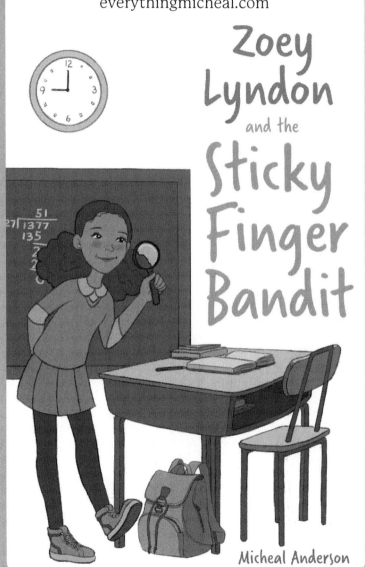

Zoey
Lyndon
and the
Sticky
Finger
Bandit

Micheal Anderson

Please write a review

Authors love hearing from their readers!

Please let Micheal Anderson know what you thought of *Zoey Lyndon and the Sticky Finger Bandit*.

Leave a review on her website **everythingmicheal.com**.

You can also leave a review on Amazon or Goodreads and this will help other children discover *Zoey Lyndon and the Sticky Finger Bandit*.

Thank You!

Micheal Anderson is an author who enjoys writing middle grade fiction and understands the value of representation in children's stories. She lives in St. Louis, Missouri with her husband and two daughters. Micheal enjoys blogging, jazz music and loves to travel abroad.

Made in the USA
Coppell, TX
08 July 2021

58707618R00083